WIND UP

ALSO BY DEREK JETER

WIND UP

DEREK JETER

with Paul Mantell

JETER CHILDREN'S

SIMON & SCHUSTER BOOKS FOR YOUNG READERS

New York   London   Toronto   Sydney   New Delhi

SIMON & SCHUSTER BOOKS FOR YOUNG READERS
An imprint of Simon & Schuster Children's Publishing Division
1230 Avenue of the Americas, New York, New York 10020
This book is a work of fiction. Any references to historical events, real people, or real places are used fictitiously. Other names, characters, places, and events are products of the author's imagination, and any resemblance to actual events or places or persons, living or dead, is entirely coincidental.
Text © 2021 by Jeter Publishing, Inc.
Cover illustration © 2021 by Tim O'Brien
Cover design by Krista Vossen © 2021 by Simon & Schuster, Inc.
All rights reserved, including the right of reproduction in whole or in part in any form.
SIMON & SCHUSTER BOOKS FOR YOUNG READERS
and related marks are trademarks of Simon & Schuster, Inc.
For information about special discounts for bulk purchases, please contact Simon & Schuster Special Sales at 1-866-506-1949 or business@simonandschuster.com.
The Simon & Schuster Speakers Bureau can bring authors to your live event.
For more information or to book an event, contact the Simon & Schuster Speakers Bureau at 1-866-248-3049 or visit our website at www.simonspeakers.com.
Also available in a Simon & Schuster Books for Young Readers hardcover edition
Interior design by Krista Vossen
The text for this book was set in Centennial.
Manufactured in the United States of America
0222 OFF
First Simon & Schuster Books for Young Readers paperback edition April 2022
2 4 6 8 10 9 7 5 3 1
Library of Congress Control Number: 2020950000
ISBN 9781534480469 (hardcover)
ISBN 9781534480452 (ebook)
ISBN 9781534480476 (pbk)

To everyone working to ensure we are healthy and safe. We are grateful for your work and sacrifices

—D. J.

A Note About the Text

The rules of Little League followed in this book are the rules of the present day. There are six innings in each game. Every player on a Little League baseball team must play at least two innings of every game in the field and have at least one at bat. In any given contest, there is a limit on the number of pitches a pitcher can throw, in accordance with age. Pitchers who are eight years old are allowed a maximum of fifty pitches in a game, pitchers who are nine or ten years old are allowed seventy-five pitches per game, and pitchers who are eleven or twelve years old are allowed eighty-five pitches.

Dear Reader,

Wind Up is inspired by some of my experiences growing up. The book portrays the values my parents instilled in me and the lessons they have taught me about how to remain true to myself and embrace the unique differences in everyone around me.

Wind Up is based on the lesson that everything in life is an opportunity both for fun and learning. This is one of the principles I have lived by in order to achieve my dreams. I hope you enjoy reading!

Derek Jeter

DEREK JETER'S 10 LIFE LESSONS

1. Set Your Goals High (*The Contract*)

2. Think Before You Act (*Hit & Miss*)

3. Deal with Growing Pains (*Change Up*)

4. The World Isn't Always Fair (*Fair Ball*)

5. Find the Right Role Models (*Curveball*)

6. Don't Be Afraid to Fail (*Fast Break*)

7. Have a Strong Supporting Cast (*Strike Zone*)

8. Be Serious but Have Fun (*Wind Up*)

9. Be a Leader, Follow the Leader

10. Life Is a Daily Challenge

CONTRACT FOR DEREK JETER

1. Family Comes First. Attend our nightly dinner.
2. Be a Role Model for Sharlee. (She looks to you to model good behavior.)
3. Do Your Schoolwork and Maintain Good Grades (As or Bs).
4. Bedtime. Lights out at nine p.m. on school nights.
5. Do Your Chores. Take out the garbage, clean your room on weekends, and help with the dishes.
6. Respect Others. Be a good friend, classmate, and teammate. Listen to your teachers, coaches, and other adults.
7. Respect Yourself. Take good care of your body and your mind. Avoid alcohol and drugs. Surround yourself with positive friends with strong values.
8. Work Hard. You owe it to yourself and those around you to give your all. Do your best in everything that you do.
9. Think Before You Act.

Failure to comply will result in the loss of playing sports and hanging out with friends. Extra-special rewards include attending a Major League Baseball game, choosing a location for dinner, and selecting another event of your choice.

CONTENTS

Chapter One

MAKE-OR-BREAK

"Goooooooooooooooo, Yanks!"

Derek Jeter felt an electric surge go through him as he and his Yankee teammates put their hands together, then lifted them skyward for their pregame cheer.

The team was at the season's final crossroads. With a win today against the Pirates, they could punch their ticket to the Little League playoffs. But if they lost, their season would be over.

Derek shuddered, picturing himself sitting around for the whole second half of June, while other kids competed for the championship.

Unthinkable! No way was Derek okay with that—not after the Yanks had come back from the dead with three straight wins, rescuing their season after a horrible start!

Today's teams were both 4–3 on the season. Not only would the losers be eliminated, but they would also finish without a winning season.

For this crucial game, Coach Stafford had switched around the Yankees' normal lineup. Instead of Harry Hicks, their usual starting pitcher, Avery Mullins was on the mound. She was the only girl on the team—or in the entire league, for that matter!

Coach K was taking a chance on Avery today because Harry had been sick with a fever earlier in the week. Derek knew she could do the job—hey, she'd done it before! On the other hand, she had never been in a game this critical.

Derek watched Avery throw her warm-up pitches. *Avery can really play some ball*, he thought. She had grit and determination, too.

Most of the guys on the team had given her a hard time at first, ignoring the fact that she'd never played organized ball before. The coaches hadn't given her much playing time, either—not until midseason, when things had already been looking desperate, and the need to shake things up had become obvious.

Still, in spite of everything, Avery was having a breakout rookie season. By now, of course, they all knew what she could do. They also knew to stay out of her way when she wasn't in the mood to fool around—like *now*.

Derek fielded a warm-up grounder and fired it over to

Ryan McDonough at first base. Then he turned and waved to his pal Vijay Patel out in right. Vijay waved back, flashing a huge grin and a victory sign.

Derek shook his head in admiration. Somehow Vijay always found a way to enjoy the moment, even under maximum pressure.

Derek wished he could take things so casually, but he couldn't. Baseball meant the world to him. One day he hoped to be the starting shortstop for the *real* New York Yankees! Every baseball game along the way meant more to him than it meant to most kids he knew.

And even though he understood that "you can't win 'em all," it was never okay with Derek when he lost.

Avery was like that too. Maybe that was why the two of them had become friends over the past month or so.

She fired one last warm-up throw, and JJ Stafford, who was the catcher and the coach's son, threw down to second base, where Pete Kozlowski, the assistant coach's son, grabbed it and put the tag on the phantom runner.

"Play ball!" shouted the umpire.

"Go, Yankees!" came a shout from the stands, louder than the general cheering.

Derek recognized his mom's voice. He turned and gave her a wave before settling into fielding position. Avery's mom was there too, along with the two teenage boys who came to all of Avery's games. Her brother's old friends, from before he'd died in the car accident.

The Pirates' leadoff man came to the plate, waggling his bat like he was going to wallop the first pitch he saw. He looked Avery up and down with a scornful smirk on his face.

Avery wound up slowly, then fired one inside and high. The hitter ducked, and catcalls came from the Pirates bench. But the batter didn't waggle his bat after that.

Avery threw one over the plate next, and the batter swung right through it. Then she tossed one low, and he grounded weakly right back to the mound. Avery grabbed it and threw to first for the easy out.

The hitter jogged back to the bench, shooting Avery a dirty look as he went. She paid no attention.

So far, so good, thought Derek. "Let's go, Avery!" he yelled, pounding his mitt.

But after that promising start, Avery's control started to waver. She walked the next batter on a 3–2 count. Then she plunked the number three hitter with a wayward fastball.

More full-out boos rose from the Pirates bench. "Throw her out!" a couple of kids yelled to the ump.

Derek blew out a worried breath. Avery had seemed stressed before the game, and he'd worried she might be feeling shaky. But he hadn't said anything to her then, and he didn't now. Avery didn't like being encouraged— not while she was in the middle of yelling at herself.

The cleanup hitter swung at the first pitch, got hold of

a high fastball, and sent it deep to center field. Mason ran back, back, back . . . *and made a sno-cone catch*!

"Let's go! Woo-hoo!" Derek yelled, raising his arms high in the air along with his teammates.

There were two out now, with the runners advancing to second and third on the play.

If Avery had felt tense before, she looked almost rigid now. She'd just thrown her best pitch, and it had been absolutely crushed. Now, seemingly scared of throwing the ball over the plate, she walked the next batter on four straight pitches to load the bases.

"No batter, no batter!" Derek called out, smacking his fist into his glove. "You got this, Ave!" She paid no attention. Derek could see her breathing hard. Her eyes looked wild as she went into her windup and fired—ball one, high.

Two pitches later, the count was 3–0. One more ball, and the Pirates would walk in a run!

"Get it over, will ya?" Pete yelled at Avery from second base. "Just throw him a strike!"

"Hey!" Derek called to him, shielding his mouth with his mitt. "Cut it out!"

Derek wished Pete would keep quiet, instead of always mouthing off at people. Did he really think yelling at her was going to help?

The next pitch was ball four—but luckily, the batter swung at it! He smacked a line drive right at Pete. But

Pete's attention was still half on Avery, and the ball caught him flat-footed. He ducked out of the way, flailing with his glove. The ball ticked off the glove and rolled onto the outfield grass!

By the time Pete had retrieved it, two runs had scored! Coach K jogged out to the mound and murmured a few words into Avery's ear. She bit her lip, shook her head, and stared hard at the ground. Coach clapped her on the shoulder and went back to the dugout.

Avery toed the rubber. She blew out a big breath, digging down deep for extra strength. *She should have been out of the inning already*, Derek thought. If only Pete had had his mind on his own job instead of hers.

"Come on, Ave . . . come on . . . ," Derek muttered. He knew she had it in her. But could she summon her ability at will?

The pitch was a low changeup. The batter swung, sending a sharp grounder to Derek's right. He dived and snagged it, rolled onto his back, and flipped to Pete at second for the final out!

Okay, so we're down 2–0. So what? Derek lectured himself. *It's not the end of the world. We haven't even come to bat yet!* He knew that no game was lost until the last out was recorded—especially in an all-or-nothing game like this one!

On the other hand, it wasn't exactly the start they'd hoped for. And the Pirates' starting pitcher was going to have a lot to say about any comebacks.

He was the hardest thrower Derek had seen all year. You could hear the menacing buzz of his fastball as it came in, looking more like a blur than a baseball.

Mason Adams, the Yanks' leadoff man, ducked out of the way of the first two pitches he saw—each of them a strike. Then he swung wildly at a fastball in the dirt—and missed by a mile.

Derek had trouble catching up with the heater too. He battled for five pitches, fouling off some good ones, but ultimately went down swinging at a changeup—the first one the pitcher had thrown.

This is going to be even tougher than I thought, Derek realized as Pete proceeded to strike out on four pitches. Derek felt a sudden tingling of anxiety as goose bumps rose on his arms.

It's 2–zip already, thought Derek. *And he threw only twelve pitches! He's still got a lot to go before he reaches his limit!*

The Yanks were going to have to make the pitcher work harder. They had to tire him out and push up his pitch count! Derek suddenly found that he was clenching his jaws. He opened his mouth wide to stretch them back out, but he could tell the situation was starting to get to him.

He wasn't the only one either. Avery hadn't said a word to anyone since the pregame group cheer. She was deep in her own thoughts. To Derek she seemed to be in agony.

He knew what Avery was like when she was relaxed

and having fun. He also knew that when she tensed up, she didn't play nearly as well.

Sure enough, having walked two batters and hit another in the previous inning, Avery threw her first pitch right down the middle of the plate.

Luckily, the batter let it go by. He was the Pirates' number eight hitter. Derek had seen him play last year and remembered him not being very athletic. Still, he was big, and if he ever got hold of one . . .

Avery's next pitch was another meatball, but this time the hitter was ready. He hit it a mile to right, way over the head of Vijay, who'd been playing shallow against the bottom of the lineup.

The Pirates bench erupted in cheers as their man lumbered into third, just ahead of the relay throw!

Seeing the Pirates jumping up and down made Avery lose her cool altogether. With a scream of rage and frustration, she threw her mitt to the ground as hard as she could, then squatted down with her head between her knees and roared again.

"Hey!" Coach K yelled at her, clapping his hands emphatically. "Get back in the game, kid! Let's hold 'em right here!"

Avery's eyes were wild with rage, and Derek knew she was furious at herself for putting the team in an early hole. She stood up and closed her eyes, took a deep breath, and rolled her shoulders around in circles.

Good, Derek thought. *She's calming herself down.*

From that moment on, Avery seemed to find her game. She threw the same pitches, but now they were catching the edges of the plate. She started mixing her speeds, which got the Pirates' hitters off-balance, taking weak hacks and missing badly.

Three strikeouts later, the Yankees ran back to the bench, feeling like they'd just dodged a bullet—and maybe even swung the momentum their way!

"Hey," Derek said as he passed Avery and they touched mitts. "Nice going there."

"Yeah, right," she muttered, looking away.

"Don't worry, Ave," he told her. "We've got 'em right where we want 'em." He grinned, to show her he meant it as a semi-joke.

She looked up at him, not even cracking a smile. "Is that supposed to be *funny?*" she asked. "Is that supposed to make me *feel better* or something?"

"Okay! Sorry I said anything," Derek told her, backing away with his hands up.

"What's going on?" Vijay asked as Derek sat down next to him. "You okay?"

"Me? I'm fine. It's Avery."

"Ah, don't take it personally. She just needs some space probably, huh?"

"I guess so. "

"Listen, though," Vijay said. "I noticed something. Did

you see in the first inning how their catcher just blocks pitches in the dirt? He doesn't even try to catch them. If we're on base, we can steal when the ball gets away!"

"I guess," Derek agreed. "That's if we can get some men on base."

"Yes. We can't be swinging at the low pitches, for sure." Vijay had a good point.

"I'm going to pass the word." Derek got up and spoke to Harry, who was leading off the inning. Then he spoke to the others, one by one.

It was good advice, though it didn't result in any runs in the second or third. Still, the Yankees, by letting the low pitches go by, were working the starter for long counts. Vijay even managed to work a walk, becoming the Yankees' first base runner.

Even though she had given up that extra-base hit to start the second, Avery had held the Pirates scoreless for three straight innings, giving up only that triple and two singles along the way. The Yankees were still down 2–0. But she'd turned her outing around, and because of that the team still had a fighting chance.

Take a strike. . . . Take a strike! Derek repeated the mantra inside his head as he stood in the batter's box, leading off the bottom of the fourth inning. He knew he was so jacked up right now, he was likely to swing at almost anything, so it was important to keep reminding himself what his job was in this situation—*to get on base.* Period.

He let a fastball go by, right down the middle for strike one. But Derek noticed that it didn't have the buzz it had had in the first inning. In fact, he was sure he could have caught up with it. *If he throws another one . . .*

He did, but it was in the dirt, and Derek just barely managed to check his swing. He proceeded to work the pitcher until he had a full count. Then Derek fouled off four straight strikes before finally being rewarded with a walk.

Success! he told himself. He was only the Yankees' second runner of the game!

Derek hoped Pete would take a strike too, since the Yanks were two runs down and needed base runners. Pete, however, was not the kind of hitter to think about those things. It was pretty much "see ball, hit ball" with him.

Luckily, he got another so-so fastball, and hit it right on the nose! Derek scooted to third, hopping to avoid the screaming grounder that easily made it past the shortstop and into left field.

Harry was up next. He'd looked weak at the plate so far—no surprise. After all, he'd been passed over as the starting pitcher today because he'd spent three days the previous week in bed with a virus. Derek could tell he still wasn't himself. Harry valiantly hung in there, making the pitcher waste seven pitches, but in the end he could only manage a weak grounder to second.

Still, that was enough for Derek. He took off like a shot for home, hoping the second baseman would try to nail him at the plate, instead of going for the easy double play.

Sure enough, the fielder took the bait. His throw home was high—and Derek slid in under the tag!

"SAFE!" yelled the ump.

Pete kept going, all the way to third! The catcher threw down there, too late, and that allowed Harry to pull into second, huffing and puffing.

One run in, men on second and third, and still nobody out! The Yankees' bench and fans were going wild. Even Avery was cheering now, although Derek noticed that she still wasn't cracking a smile as she stepped into the left-handed batter's box.

The pitcher threw one into the dirt for a ball. Suddenly the ump called time and signaled to the Pirates' coach. "That's eighty-five," Derek heard the ump say. "I'll take the ball, son," he told the frustrated starter.

The Pirates' new pitcher was a lefty, Derek noticed. He wondered if their coach had put him in just to pitch to the left-hitting Avery.

If so, they were in for a shock. After watching the new kid throw his warm-up pitches, Avery calmly walked around to the right-handed batter's box and took a few practice swings.

Derek smiled as he saw the coach's eyes go wide with surprise. A switch-hitter! *Oh, well,* Derek thought with amusement. There was nothing the coach could do about it now.

Avery let one pitch go by, taking a strike. She might have been new to playing ball, but for years she'd watched every game her older brother had played. He'd been headed for a college baseball scholarship—until the car crash. That had been a year ago. Now Avery was playing to honor his memory. Derek knew that was why she took it so hard when things went badly.

Avery let another pitch go by, a ball that evened the count at 1–1. Then she lined a fastball right back at the pitcher, who ducked, protecting his face with his mitt.

Incredibly, the ball stuck right in it! Realizing he'd caught it, the pitcher threw quickly to second, where the shortstop tagged Harry before he could get back to the base.

Double play!

"NOOOOO!" Avery screamed in fury, smacking her bat hard onto the plate, then kicking the dirt before heading back to the bench.

There was no consoling her. She angrily shook off pats on the back, then plunked herself down at the very end of the bench, alone and despairing.

"Hey, we're not done yet!" Derek called out, meaning it for her, even though he didn't dare look her way.

Ryan came to the plate, with Pete on third and two out. Ryan was their season RBI leader, and once again he came through in the clutch—lashing a double down the left field line! Pete scored easily to tie the game, 2–2.

After JJ popped out to end the inning, Coach K offered Avery the ball. "You good for one more inning?" he asked. She nodded, took the ball from him, and marched out to the mound for the top of the fifth.

After getting the first two outs, though, she seemed to tire. Her pitches were all over the place again, like in the first inning. She walked two, then gave up a double that scored both the Pirates' runners!

Coach K walked slowly to the mound, took the ball from her, and motioned for Harry to come in from third to pitch. Tre' entered the game to play third, and Avery walked slowly to the dugout, never once looking up from the ground. She sat down so heavily that it seemed to Derek she never meant to get up again.

He wanted to tell her that he understood, that he was feeling a different version of the same thing. He wanted to tell her not to give up, that the Yanks still had plenty of fight left, and that a 4–2 deficit wasn't an impossible mountain to climb—not with six outs left!

But there was no time to talk. Harry was done warming up, and the game was about to resume.

Harry threw one pitch, and it was enough. The hitter smashed it just to Derek's right. He snagged it, planted his foot, and threw a BB to first for the final Pirates out of the inning!

In their half of the fifth, the Yankees brought the bottom of their batting order to the plate, to face yet another Pirates pitcher—a righty this time. Derek saw that this one's pitches started off looking good but then faded, winding up in the dirt. They looked tempting, but they were more like fish bait.

After two strikes, the Pirates' pitcher finished Elliott off with a high floater that dropped in for a third strike. Derek took careful note.

"Hey, Vij," he said to his friend in the on-deck circle. "Don't bite on those fastballs. Wait for the high, slow pitch."

Vijay gave Derek a nod and a wink as he walked to the plate.

"Come on, Vij," Derek muttered under his breath. "Keep it going, man. . . . Get me an at bat."

Vijay took two balls in the dirt, then swung hard at the floater. He cued it off the end of the bat—just a dribbler, really—but it took a crazy bounce, and Vijay wound up beating the throw, for a single!

Derek clued Mason in too, and he worked a walk. Suddenly, with men on first and second, it was all up to Derek!

This time he didn't just need to get on base. He didn't need to take a strike. He needed to hit one as hard as he could and tie up this game!

The first pitch he saw was the floater—the pitcher had obviously decided to trick him by changing his pattern.

Derek waited on it, then leaned in and whacked it to left.

He took off running like a shot. Vijay and Mason raced around to score ahead of him, and Derek wound up on third with a super-clutch, game-tying triple!

The Yankees and their fans were going wild with excitement. Even Avery was up and shouting now.

Derek could feel the blood pounding in his head. He'd done it! Now, if only they could finish the Pirates off . . .

The pitcher, clearly rattled, hit Pete in the butt with a slow curve. Pete yowled comically, rubbing the sore spot as he limped to first. The Yankees laughed and clapped, enjoying themselves now. The Pirates, meanwhile, stood staring glumly as their playoff dreams evaporated before their eyes.

Harry put the icing on the cake by creaming a double to right, scoring Derek and Pete easily! Even though Tre', hitting for Avery, then grounded into a double play to end the inning, it was now 6–4, Yanks! Only three outs to go to nail down a playoff spot!

Harry proceeded to take care of business, finally looking like his old, healthy self in retiring three discouraged Pirates in a row to seal the victory.

All the Yankees rejoiced together. To Derek, it was as if a ten-ton weight had been lifted off his shoulders. Whatever happened next, at least they'd made the playoffs. No one could say their season had been a failure.

He looked over at Avery, who was finally smiling. "Hey,

you! Up top!" he said, and she gladly high-fived him. They even exchanged hugs, as if the tension and testiness had never existed.

"You okay?" he asked.

Her smile vanished, replied by a quizzical look. "What are you talking about?" She looked at him like he was crazy.

"Uh . . . nothing. Forget it," said Derek, shrugging. "Great game, huh?"

"Hey, we made it," she said. "That's all that matters!"

Derek let it go at that. Whatever her problem had been, she seemed all right now. He went to find his mom and celebrate some more.

Chapter Two

STRESS TEST

"All right, class—listen up, please."

Derek turned his attention to the front of the room. The bell for last period had just rung. Ms. Terrapin was rapping on her desk with a ruler, and the class had now quieted down enough for her to continue.

"I'm going to hand out the schedule for finals," she said, picking up a sheaf of papers and handing a few to each student in the front row. "Pass them back, please. Now, don't panic," she added. "Your class presentations in social studies and foreign language will be counted as your finals in those subjects, so it's just math, English, and science you'll have to bone up on."

Sighs of relief greeted this happy news. "HOWEVER,"

Ms. Terrapin went on, "there's a new twist this year. As I told you back in January, you'll also be taking the national standardized tests."

A worried murmur rose from the four corners of the room. Derek vaguely remembered her saying something about standardized tests, a long, long time ago—but he'd let himself forget all about them. He'd taken them before—way back in fourth grade—and the one thing he remembered was that his teacher had told Derek's parents not to worry that he hadn't scored as well as he usually did on his finals, that he'd probably just had "test anxiety."

"Hey, Jeter! Where're you running? C'mere a minute."

Derek looked back over his shoulder to see Gary Parnell emerging from the classroom. Gary approached him, a sinister grin on his face.

Uh-oh, thought Derek. Whatever that grin signified, it could not possibly be good. "What's up, Gary?" he asked, trying to sound casual.

"I think you already know—don't you?" It wasn't even really a question. "Of course you do. It's time for our annual finals challenge!" He rubbed his two hands together eagerly. "I, for one, can't wait! You?"

"Joy," said Derek sarcastically.

Gary had been in Derek's class every year since second grade. Every year, Gary had challenged Derek to a contest—whoever got the highest grades on their finals won. And the loser had to pay a price.

"I figure since we're bigger this year, we should have bigger penalties," Gary said. "Don't you agree?" The grin grew wider.

"Totally," Derek said, trying to shoot a cocky smile back at Gary and wondering if it looked cocky enough.

"Of course, if you'd rather not compete this year . . ."

"Not compete?"

"I mean, I could understand. I've had another year to leapfrog your pathetic intelligence. It probably wouldn't even be a fair fight—"

"You're on!" Derek said hotly, even as he wished he'd kept his mouth shut. Gary almost always got better grades than Derek did. The few times when he'd beaten Gary had only served to keep Derek in the game for future punishments.

"Seriously?" Gary said, raising his eyebrows in surprise. "You actually think you can win this thing?"

"I *know* I can."

"Then how about this for a penalty—on the last morning of school, the loser has to write on every classroom blackboard, 'Gary Parnell is smarter than I am.' And sign it."

"You mean 'Derek Jeter is smarter,'" Derek corrected him. "Sounds good." A hysterically funny idea crossed his mind, at the same time that he felt an urge to stick it to Gary. Those two things combined at that fateful moment to make Derek say something he would soon come to regret:

"And I'll go you one better. Whoever loses has to dress up in a chicken suit the last day of school!"

"Oooo . . . I like it!" Gary said, rubbing his hands together some more. "I can't wait, Jeter. You are dead meat—I've always killed on standardized tests."

"W-wait. Who said we were counting those?" Derek asked, suddenly thrown off-balance.

Gary shrugged. "They're part of our finals, aren't they? So there we are—best three out of five. Since you're so baseball crazy, think of it as an academic 'World Series.' Unless, of course, you want to back out. In which case—"

"No way," Derek said, thrusting out his hand. "You've got yourself a deal."

"I shouldn't have agreed to include the standardized tests," Derek said to Vijay as the two friends rode the school bus home to Mount Royal Townhouses.

"Don't worry," Vijay told him. "You will beat him. You'll see."

"Did I say I was worried?"

"It's not what you said. It's the look on your face."

"What look?" Derek asked, a little irritated.

Vijay chuckled. "Never mind. Look, the standardized tests are a snap. No problem for you."

"How do you know that?"

"You're one of the smartest kids in school. Trust me,

I know what I'm talking about. I am very experienced with these kinds of tests. My parents had me do a whole battery of them when we came here from India. I think they wanted to show people I was not behind in my schooling."

Derek laughed. "Behind? That's funny."

"So with all my experience, I can help you practice for them," Vijay offered.

"You would do that?"

"Sure! It will be fun to study together. And even more fun watching Gary wear a chicken suit!"

Derek laughed. Somehow, as he always did, his old friend had found a way to make Derek feel better. Just the thought of Vijay and his big brain helping him study gave Derek hope.

The bus pulled into the Mount Royal stop, and the two boys got off. "See you at four thirty?" Vijay asked.

"I'll be there," Derek told him. "Aren't I always?"

One good thing about finals coming up was that Derek's teacher had let them off the hook as far as homework was concerned.

"Seriously?" his dad asked, raising a doubtful eyebrow.

"Dad," Derek said, tilting his head, "not only finals but standardized tests, too!"

"I see," said Mr. Jeter, who was going through a pile of work he'd brought home from his office. "And how much time did you just put into studying?"

"An hour and fifteen minutes. Dad, my brain can't take in any more right now. Please?"

"Are you off to the Hill, then?"

"Yup. Thanks, Dad!" Derek said, rushing to the hall closet to grab his mitt and bat.

"Say hi to everybody," said his dad as Derek flew out the door. "Especially Vijay and Dave. Tell them good luck in the playoffs."

Derek heard that last part as he pulled the front door closed behind him. He set off at a run, headed for the open slope in the middle of Mount Royal Townhouses that all the kids called Derek Jeter's Hill.

And why shouldn't they name it after him? Derek practically lived there. Hardly a day went by when he wasn't already waiting for whoever else happened to show up to play ball.

With stones and protruding tree roots for bases, and the occasional bush as an obstacle in the outfield, the Hill posed its challenges. But it was the only field of any kind close enough for the kids' parents to still be within shouting distance.

There were already lots of kids out there, playing and taking fielding practice. One of Avery's older friends, from her neighborhood, was hitting grounders and flies to the others. The local field in Avery's neighborhood was under renovation, so those kids had all shifted over here, making the Hill more crowded than it used to be.

But Derek liked it—it meant they had enough kids to play real games. Avery's friends had all been close to her brother—and, well, Derek *liked* playing with older kids. It brought out the best in his game.

He spotted Avery, fielding a hot grounder at second and flipping it back in. She waved to Derek, and he waved back. "Get out here!" she called. "I need my double-play partner!"

That was more like it—the usual Avery, relaxed and fun, and still as tough as nails.

Derek grinned, dropped his bat next to the backstop, and ran out to take his place at short.

Vijay came running down the path, waving as he took his place in right field—just in time to field a fly ball hit his way.

Derek looked around, shielding his eyes from the sun, trying to see if Dave had arrived yet. Dave was Derek's other best friend. Except that lately they hadn't seen each other as much as usual.

Dave had been on Derek's previous Little League teams, but not this year. And that meant they had different schedules, different practices—not to mention they were in different classes at school this year too.

That's weird, thought Derek. *He said he'd be here. . . .* It wasn't like Dave to say he'd be someplace and then not show. And it wasn't like he couldn't get a ride for some reason. Dave's family was rich and had their own driver, Chase Bradway, who was also Dave's guardian. Chase looked after Dave whenever his mom and dad were away, which was most of the time. So Dave always had a lift to get wherever he needed.

Something must have come up. But what?

This was no time to think about it, though. They were already choosing sides for a pickup game.

Soon it was in full swing. And Derek approached every game like it was the seventh game of the World Series. Nothing else got in the way when he was on the field or at the plate, or even just watching the game from the bench.

Avery was the same way. But here on the Hill, where the stakes weren't as high, she didn't seem to stress out as much. And like most people, she played even better when she played loose.

About midway through the game, one of Avery's older friends hit a screaming one-hopper to Derek's right. He took two running steps, then dived for it—and skidded a full six feet on a bare patch scattered with sharp gravel.

Ouch. Ow . . . ow . . . He got up slowly, dusting off his chest and legs. The ribs on his right side burned, and he knew he'd skinned himself badly.

"You okay?" Avery called to him from second base.

"I'm fine," he said, tensing his jaw and pounding his glove. He knew he wasn't fine. But he was okay enough to go on playing. Derek was not going to let a mere flesh wound get him out of the game. Still, he knew it was going to take some tending to when he got home.

But what bothered him worse than his scratched ribs was Dave not showing up. It wasn't like him, especially when he'd said only that day at lunch that he'd be there.

"Wouldn't miss it!" Derek remembered him saying. "Not many more times we can get on a ball field together before school's out and you head off to New Jersey." As in Derek's grandparents' house, where he and Sharlee spent all their summers.

So what had happened to Dave?

Chapter Three

SERIOUS BUSINESS

"Whoa. That's some strawberry you've got there. It must sting pretty good, huh?" Derek's mom was staring at his ribs. At least the scratches weren't deep, and hadn't bled a lot. "Here, let me wash that and get some triple antibiotic cream on it."

She got out a clean washcloth, ran it under warm water, came back to the bedroom, and gently dabbed at the wounds. Derek breathed in sharply, hissing as the burning sensation hit him.

"I dived for a liner, out on the Hill," he told her.

She shook her head and let out a chuckle. "Did you at least make the play?"

Derek shook his head. "That's what *really* hurts," he said, managing a wincing grin.

She got out some gauze and taped over his wounds, then helped him with his pajama top. "So, how's school going?" she asked.

"Huh?"

"You know—*school*? Where you go five days a week?"

"Oh. It's fine," Derek said.

"I can see you've got other things on your mind." She sat on the edge of the bed next to him. "Want to talk about it?"

Derek shrugged and sighed. "I don't know. It's just . . . we've got our first playoff game coming up, and there's a bunch of teams with better records than us. . . ."

"And . . . ?"

"I just wish Dad was coaching *us* instead of Sharlee's team. Like last year, when we won it all. With him as our coach, we just *knew* we were going to win. But without him . . . ?"

"This year it was Sharlee's turn," she reminded him. "And by the way, old man—and I know your dad would agree—remember that it was you kids who went out there and played your hearts out and won that trophy, not him. And it's going to be the same this time around."

Derek shook his head. "I just feel a lot more nervous about it this year," he admitted. "And I'm not the only one. Avery's a mess. Pete's losing his cool. . . ."

"Poor Avery. I know how much this means to her, with her brother and all."

Derek nodded. Avery's big brother had taught her the game, and she'd idolized him, much like Derek idolized his dad.

"And there's something else," Derek told his mom. "Dave didn't show up to play on the Hill today."

Mrs. Jeter shrugged. "Something probably came up."

"It's never happened before. And he said he'd be there!"

"Don't worry, old man. I'm sure it's nothing serious." She kissed Derek on the forehead. "Now try to get some sleep."

"Ow!" Derek said as he realized that lying on his left side was too painful. He turned over, got comfortable, and said, "G'night," as she turned out the light.

"Remember, Derek—no matter what happens, it's still a game."

"Meaning what?"

"Meaning that if you're not having fun, what's the point?"

After the tension of his last ball game, Derek could relate. Both he and Avery, not to mention a number of his other teammates, had all played tight as the pressure had built to a boiling point.

Derek understood what his mom was getting at. But it was hard to relax and stay loose when he had so much on his mind.

As he lay there in the dark, he wondered whether Dave had purposely stayed away, knowing that if their teams kept winning, they were on a collision course to meet in the final round.

Could that be it? Derek wondered.

Or maybe it was about *Avery.*

Ever since Derek and Vijay had made friends with her, they'd seen less and less of Dave. Partly that was because Dave was on a different team. But Derek remembered that Dave had been weirded out at first, dealing with the fact that a girl was now part of their regular get-togethers.

Avery was definitely part of their tight-knit gang now. The question was, *was Dave?*

From the moment when he woke up on Saturday, Derek was in a bad mood. First of all, his ribs still stung pretty badly. Second of all, Dave didn't call all morning.

Derek started studying for finals, but he just couldn't keep his mind on his work. He tried math, science, history, English—it didn't matter the subject. Nothing was sinking in, and it was only making him more irritable.

Finally he'd put in the studying time he'd promised his parents—a minimum of one hour a day. As part of the contract they'd drawn up together and Derek had signed, he had to abide by a strict set of rules—one of which was that he had to finish his daily homework before going out to play ball or hang out with friends.

But today it was raining hard, and Coach Stafford

had called midmorning to say that their game was now rescheduled for Wednesday at four o'clock. That would give Derek time to heal. But it would also give him more time to worry about everything.

It didn't help that Sharlee was in such a state of happy excitement and refused to leave him alone to sulk.

"You'll never guess the surprise!" she teased, coming up behind him as he sat on the couch, watching the Tigers play the Red Sox in sunny Boston.

"Just tell me already," he said, rolling his eyes as he looked away from her.

"I *can't* tell you!" she said with a giggle. "What kind of surprise would that be? Besides, your birthday isn't for two more weeks!"

"Are you going to torment me about it for two weeks?" he asked, raising his eyebrows so that she laughed again.

"Yes!" she said. "Come on, guess!"

"If I guess right, you'll be upset."

"You'll *never* guess."

"Then why make me try?" he asked. "Oh, wait. I know. To drive me crazy, right?"

"Right! And by the way, you're coming to my next game, right?"

"Of course, duh," he said. "But right now I'm actually watching a *different* game. So unless you want to watch with me . . ."

"Derek," his father said, looking up from his newspaper

as he sat in the easy chair opposite the sofa. "That's enough now."

"I'm going to hit a home run for you," Sharlee promised, leaning in and whispering it right into his ear.

"Is that the surprise?" he asked.

"Huh? That's not a surprise. I hit a home run *every* game!"

She did, too, Derek knew. Sharlee was quite an athlete. And she couldn't help it if her excitement irritated him. She was simply having fun, like their mom said was the whole point of playing.

Mrs. Jeter came in just then and placed a bowl of freshly popped popcorn on the coffee table. "Mommy!" Sharlee cried, throwing her arms around her. Then Derek heard her whisper to their mom, "Let's go work on our surprise!" Sharlee shot a cunning glance at Derek.

"Ohhh, so it's something you're cooking up *together*!" Derek said. "Sharlee, you'd better watch out—I'm going to worm it out of you yet." He reached over and tickled her. She hid behind their mom, giggling, then pulled their mother away into the kitchen.

Finally, thought Derek. Now he could watch the game in peace.

"Derek," said his dad, lowering his newspaper and giving him a serious look.

"Huh?"

"I didn't like how you were talking to your sister just now."

"What'd I say?"

"It was your tone of voice, Son. I think you came pretty close to hurting Sharlee's feelings."

"She was fine!" Derek protested.

"*This* time. But maybe not next time. In any case, remember, it says in your contract—read it again—to always treat your family and *all* people with respect. I didn't hear respect in your tone just then. I let it go, just to see if you'd stop on your own, and you did."

Derek was silent. He knew his dad was right.

"I know you're sorry about it, and I don't expect to hear that tone from you again. Understand?"

"Yes, Dad."

"Now, if you want to talk about what's making you so thin-skinned, I'm listening," said Mr. Jeter.

"I'm sorry, Dad," Derek said. "I don't know why I got so annoyed. I've just been . . . I don't know . . . tense lately."

"Well, I guess it's understandable. Finals coming up, playoffs coming up. Just remember—two more weeks, and all of that will be over. But your sister will be around a whole lot longer."

"Yes, Dad."

"Summer will be here before you know it. Meanwhile, try to find ways to relax and enjoy the moment."

Derek knew his dad was right. His mom had told him pretty much the same thing.

So why was it so hard for him to *actually do it*?

Chapter Four

EARTHQUAKE

Derek's ribs felt better the next morning. After two hours of review for his tests and a break for lunch, he asked if he could be excused to go play ball.

"How's that injury of yours?" asked his mom. "Sure you're okay to play?"

"It's fine," Derek said, causing his mom to raise an eyebrow.

"In that case, you're a fast healer," she said. "Well, be careful out there. Don't make it worse. No diving for balls, okay?"

"Mom," Derek said, raising his own eyebrows in return. "I'll be back for dinner." He kissed her on the cheek and was out the door, headed for the Hill.

He thought he knew now what had really been on his mind the past two days. Not the upcoming playoff game on Wednesday. Not his finals bet with Gary. Those things were on his mind, sure. But what was really eating at him was *Dave*.

As Derek neared the field, he saw that once again Dave was missing in action.

The vague sense of unease that had been eating at him all weekend suddenly grew into a wave of outright foreboding. *What could possibly be going on?*

Derek tried to put his worries aside and have fun. The kids got a game started, and soon Derek started feeling a little more at ease. But maybe that relaxed feeling was just a mirage—because he booted the first grounder that came his way—something he rarely did.

The embarrassment of blowing an easy play made him shake off his worries and really concentrate on the moment. The game kept him busy until five thirty, when it was time to go home for dinner. As he was rounding the bend in the path at the corner of his building, he stopped short.

There, parked outside the Jeters' townhouse, was the familiar black sedan, with Chase sitting behind the wheel. Standing on the sidewalk next to it was Dave—and from the glum look on his face, Derek knew right away that something major was wrong and he hadn't been worried over nothing after all.

"Hi," Derek said. *Uh-oh. Here it comes,* he thought.

"Sorry I didn't make it on Friday," said Dave, looking down at the ground.

"Or today."

"Or today." Dave heaved a big sigh. "Sorry." He looked like he was about to cry. "It's just—" Another big sigh, and Dave stared up at the clouds. "We're moving."

"Huh?"

"My mom and dad and I. We're *moving*."

Derek felt the ground suddenly shift beneath his feet. His stomach heaved. *"What? When?"*

"Soon as school's over," Dave said.

"Where?"

Dave brought his gaze down to look right at Derek. "You're not going to believe it."

"Try me," said Derek.

"Hong Kong."

"No way!"

"Way."

"I can't believe this."

"Told you. Me neither—it's crazy, right?"

"What happened? Why are you moving?"

"My mom's job got transferred," Dave explained. "She's got a two-year posting at the firm's Hong Kong office, and my dad's going to start his own company to operate out of China."

"This totally stinks!" Derek said. "*Two years?* And then what? You're coming back here?"

Dave shrugged and shook his head. "Who knows? We've moved before, a bunch of times. But I really thought this time was going to be it. 'The last move'—that's what they said then."

"Poor you," Derek said. However hard this was for him, it was going to be a lot harder for Dave.

"I know. I've been so bummed out about it ever since they told me. That's why I didn't show up on Friday . . . or today. I've just been trying to deal with it . . . you know? It isn't easy."

"Man." Derek shook his head. "A foreign country? All new kids? Who knows if they'll even speak English!"

"Oh, they will," Dave assured him. "My parents are putting me in an international school, with kids from all over. They teach in English, so it's a good bet all the kids speak it."

"Well," said Derek. "At least there's that."

"Yeah, but it's like, I've got to start all over again—*again*. Every time we move, I've got a new school to get used to, I've got to make new friends from scratch—I'm sick of it!"

No wonder Dave's friendships here in Kalamazoo were so precious to him, Derek realized. No wonder he was so upset!

Chase rolled the driver's window down. "You okay, Dave?" he asked. "Hi, Derek."

"Hi, Chase," Derek said. "I guess you're leaving too, huh?"

"No, not me. The Hennums want me to stay and look after the house. And they'll be around more for Dave over there, so . . ."

Derek suddenly felt the weight of this new reality pressing down on him. Chase must have sensed how he felt, because he added, "You know, two years isn't really that long; you have your whole lives ahead of you. In the meantime, you guys can write to each other, even call once in a while. It doesn't have to be the end of the world."

Derek nodded, but he had a hard time believing it. Two years might as well be forever. By that time, Dave would have made all-new friends. And who knew if the Hennums would move back to Kalamazoo?

"We've got to get back, Dave. Your folks said six o'clock for dinner."

"I've got to go too," Derek said. "See you tomorrow in school?"

Dave nodded, still looking at the ground. Derek turned and went inside. He heard the car door shut, and the sedan drive off. He closed the front door, as if he were closing it on his past life and leaving it behind forever.

Chapter Five

END OF THE LINE?

"I'm so excited for my game, Derek! Aren't you?"

"I am *so* excited, Sharlee. Very, *very* excited. I'll be even *more* excited for you on Wednesday, when the game actually happens."

Derek looked up from his math textbook. Sharlee was staring over his shoulder at the pile of review papers scattered around him on the coffee table.

"You don't *sound* excited," she said, pouting. "You sound annoyed."

"Sorry," he said sincerely. "I'm not annoyed. Not at you. More at life."

"Huh?"

"Ah, forget it. It's not important."

"Well, my game is important. You could at least pretend you were excited about it."

"Aw, come on, Sharlee. I really *am* excited—for *both* of us. But you know I've got a game on Wednesday myself."

"You mean you can't come to my game? Again?"

"Can I help it if we both have games at the same time? I don't make up the schedules."

"Can't you just skip your game and come see mine? Pleeeeze?"

"You know I can't, Sharlee. Remember, my team's in the playoffs. It isn't every year you get a shot at a championship."

Sharlee seemed taken aback. "Yes, it is," she insisted. "My teams win every single year."

"So far. One of these years, you might not."

"That's just silly."

"Sharlee, didn't anyone ever tell you that you can't win 'em all?"

"No," she said, shaking her head and grinning. "And I wouldn't believe them anyway. You never think you're going to lose!"

"Well, I've been on teams that didn't go to the playoffs, so . . ."

"Yeah, but that's *you,* not *me.*"

"Well, there you go. I can't argue with that. Case closed." Derek tickled her ribs, and she ran off, giggling.

Then she came back, keeping a safe distance. "What is all this mess, anyway?"

"It's for school. Big tests coming up."

"But it's Sunday night, Derek! Aren't you done studying yet?"

Derek shook his head and sighed. "Not yet," he confessed.

"You're being so boring!" she said, turning and heading for the kitchen. "I'm going to see if Mommy wants to play."

Derek would rather have been playing with her than trying to pound numbers into his skull. His brain was so stressed, it was hard to concentrate on anything!

He still hadn't told his parents about Dave. They'd asked him what was wrong over dinner, but he'd said he didn't want to talk about it.

Derek shut his textbook, piled the mess of papers on top of it, and carried the whole stack upstairs to his room. "You okay, old man?" his mother called after him. He turned back to look at her and saw that Sharlee was clinging to her leg, dragging her toward the living room to play.

"I'm not feeling too well," Derek said. "I'm going to go to bed."

"Oh dear. I'll come up in a little while and see you." Then, "Don't pull, Sharlee. I'm coming."

Derek washed up and got ready for bed. He had no energy at all, as if something had been drained out of him. He must have been lying on his back for a full half hour before he heard his mom's soft knock on the door. "Come in," he said.

"Still not feeling well?" She took one look at him and

answered her own question. "What's wrong, honey? What happened?"

Derek told her, feeling a lump rising in his throat.

"Oh, Derek." She hugged him as they sat side by side on the edge of the bed. "That's a hard blow. Really hard. I'm so sorry."

She gave him a little squeeze, then let go. "But you know, it doesn't have to mean the end of your friendship. If you two both want to stay friends, you can make it happen."

"By writing letters?" Derek asked. "That's what Chase said too. But I don't know. . . . I've never been much good at writing stuff."

"You've never had to be!" she said. "But if you knew it would help you stay friends, and stay in touch till you see each other again, why wouldn't you do it?"

"I guess."

"There you go." Giving him a kiss on the forehead, she added, "Now, good night, early bird. Feel better in the morning."

"Thanks, Mom."

Lying in bed, Derek pictured himself sitting at a desk, writing Dave a long letter, telling him everything that was happening—all the games on the Hill, school stuff, the basketball team this fall . . .

Dave wouldn't be there for that, either. They'd been looking forward to being starters together on the Friars in September.

Well, thought Derek, if it meant he had a chance to stay friends with Dave, he would sit down and write letters, whether he liked doing it or not.

But what about Dave? Would *he* be willing to go to all that trouble?

Derek had just gotten off the bus Monday morning when he saw the black sedan pull up to the curb in front of the school. Dave got out and shut the door behind him. He slowly trudged toward the school's main entrance, looking neither left nor right, but only straight ahead, into the far distance. His feet shuffled as he walked, which certainly wasn't normal for him, and he slouched forward, like a defeated soldier limping home after a battle.

He looks like a zombie! Derek couldn't help thinking.

Derek tried to get through the crowd of kids to see if his friend was okay. As bad as Derek had felt the night before—and he only felt slightly better this morning—Dave certainly seemed to be taking things much, much worse!

But it was impossible to get through the mass of kids funneling through the front doors, hurrying to get to class before the bell sounded. Derek watched Dave's head disappear down the hallway and around the corner. *I'll have to find him at lunch*, he told himself.

• • •

That morning, as the class reviewed for finals, Gary's snide whispered comments, which usually amused Derek, irritated him far more than usual.

How was he supposed to concentrate under these circumstances?

The morning went from bad to worse when Ms. Terrapin handed out practice standardized tests, along with number two pencils, so they could practice against the time clock.

Derek's anxiety caused him to put too much pressure on his pencil, and the point quickly broke off, which meant he had to get out his pencil sharpener and make a new point.

This kept happening, and half the time the pencil left marks in the wrong circles, which Derek had to erase, leaving smudges, costing precious time, and—*UGGHH!*

He didn't have to glance to his left to see the amused look on Gary's face. He just knew it was there.

Derek could have kicked himself now for accepting Gary's dare! Of course, he'd never been one to shrink from a challenge.

But he couldn't have foreseen the news about Dave. And that changed everything.

For the second time that week, he caught himself grinding his teeth.

Derek found Dave in the cafeteria. He was sitting alone at a table in the far corner, taking the occasional bite out of his sandwich, and slowly chewing it while staring into space. Derek plopped his tray down and sat next to him.

"Man, this stinks," Derek said, not feeling much like eating.

"You can say that again," Dave agreed. "I was so mad! For two days I just wouldn't talk to my folks. I even threatened to fail my finals on purpose."

"Wow!" Derek was shocked that Dave would go so far.

"Chase finally calmed me down. I mean, he was right. It's not my parents' fault. It's just the kind of work they do. And there's nothing I can do to change it anyway, so what's the point of punishing myself, right?"

"Right."

"But it still doesn't make me feel any better," Dave said, putting his sandwich down instead of biting into it. "You want this? I'm not hungry."

"No, thanks," said Derek, who was barely eating his own lunch. "I feel crummy too."

"I've been trying to study, but I just can't concentrate."

"Me neither."

"Yeah, but you're not the one who's moving. It's not as hard for you."

"Do you think Chase is right?" Derek asked. "I mean, what he said about writing to each other?"

Dave stared straight ahead, but he wasn't really looking at anything. "I don't know," he said. "That's what my old friends and I promised each other when I moved here."

"And?"

Dave shrugged. "One or two of them still write now and then, and I write back, but . . ."

"But what?"

Dave turned to look at Derek, a hopeless expression on his face. "But I've never seen any of them since we moved. Not a single one."

Chapter Six

PLAYOFF FEVER

When Derek and Vijay arrived at Westwood Fields after school that Wednesday, Derek saw that the Reds were already out there, taking fielding practice. *They sure got here early,* he thought.

"I'll go park," said Mrs. Jeter as she pulled up to the curb. "See you out there, boys. Go get 'em."

"Thanks, Mrs. Jeter!" said Vijay.

"Thanks, Mom."

Derek grabbed his mitt and jumped out of the station wagon, then swung the door shut behind him. As he and Vijay jogged over to meet their teammates, Derek noticed that the Reds were making some sparkling plays in the field.

This was not going to be easy. The Reds had finished the regular season 5–3, the same record as the Yankees. But the Reds had beaten them head-to-head during the season, so that meant the Reds finished fourth, ahead of the Yanks. Which also made the Reds the home team today.

Whichever team took this wild-card game would win the "big prize"—a matchup against the undefeated first-place Giants in the next round.

Meanwhile, Dave's Tigers and the Marlins, tied for second place with identical 6–2 records, would meet up to decide the other finalist.

Derek understood why the Reds were here early, getting extra practice in before the big game. It had originally been scheduled for last Saturday, but the rain had forced them all to wait . . . and wait. If it had been up to Derek, he and the Yankees would have been here since dawn this morning.

He greeted his teammates, then looked around for Avery. There she was, coming down the block, with her mom and two of Avery's brother's friends who'd been to nearly every game this season.

The sun was behind her, and Derek squinted to keep the sun out of his eyes. Wait . . . was she walking funny? She seemed almost to double over once or twice, grabbing her stomach.

By the time she'd reached the Yankees bench, though, she seemed okay. She high-fived the rest of the kids as usual, not cracking a smile. Then she sat down at the end of the bench, staring out at the field, a baseball in her hands. *All business.*

Derek wondered if he should go over and see if she was okay, but if she was getting her head ready for the game, he didn't want to interrupt.

Had he *imagined* her wincing in pain like that? Maybe it had just been the sun in his eyes.

Turning his attention back to the Reds, Derek could see that they were a tight-knit team. They all worked well together, encouraging one another at every turn—even in practice.

Good coaching, Derek thought, feeling a wave of worry come over him. The Yankees had walked a tightrope for the entire second half of the season to get here. They hadn't dominated any single game they'd played. They'd come close to losing so many times—and yet, here they were.

Was this going to be the day their luck ran out?

Derek shook off the feelings that were trying to invade his brain. *No way,* he told himself. *Not if I have anything to say about it!*

It wasn't just fielding that made the Reds tick—their starting pitcher was really tough. His pitches had all kinds of movement. Derek was the only Yankee to hit a fair ball in the first inning—a weak pop-up to second. Mason had fouled out to lead off, and Pete struck out to end it—one, two, three.

In the bottom of the first, the Reds, who were not a particularly big team size-wise, surprised Derek by tee-ing off on Harry's fastballs for three straight hits and two quick runs! With a runner on second, nobody out, and the cleanup hitter coming up, Derek found himself getting nervous, a cold sweat breaking out on his forehead.

Luckily, the cleanup man smacked a line drive right up the middle—right to where Derek was playing him, because the hitter was left-handed. Derek snagged it and stepped on second to double up the runner, who had started for third on contact. Two outs, and nobody on!

The number five hitter kept the pressure on, though, doubling to Vijay in right. Derek looked in at Harry, who seemed half-defeated, confused by his inability to get the ball past the hitters.

Derek jogged quickly to the mound. "Mix it up more, Har," Derek told him in a low voice. "They're onto your fastball." Then he got back into position, ready for any-thing.

Harry threw a big, fat changeup. Derek was right—the hitter was keyed to the fastball and swung way too early. The bat barely touched the ball, and it landed right in front of JJ, the catcher, who grabbed it and threw to first to end the threat.

"That-a-way, Harry!" Derek shouted, raising his hands

over his head. But Harry only shook his head in reply, exasperated with himself.

As he was watching his team hit again in the second, Derek found his tension meter rising again. Vijay, sitting next to him on the bench, must have noticed, because he said, "Only two runs—no problem. We've got this, right, Derek?"

"Totally," Derek said, forcing himself to think positive.

"Hey, loosen up!" Vijay said, hearing the doubt in Derek's voice. "What's up with you? Your shoulders are so tense, they're scrunched right up to your ears!"

"Huh?" Derek suddenly realized it was true. Without noticing it, he'd scrunched himself up into a ball of muscle. "Wow. I see what you mean."

He rolled his head around in a circle, trying to get the kinks out of his neck. Then he rolled his shoulders around, to loosen them up too. "Thanks, Vij," he said. "I don't know what's going on with me today."

But he *did* know. At least he *thought* he did. It was the news about Dave that had shaken him up, thrown him off his game.

"No problem," Vijay said with a smile. "Like I said, we've got this, right?"

"Right!" Derek replied. And this time he really meant it.

Then he looked over at Avery, who was sitting on the bench, rocking back and forth and biting her nails. He'd seen her like that a few times before, in tense moments of earlier games. But this time it looked like she was in actual physical *pain*. She seemed to almost be wincing.

He was about to go over and demand that she tell him what was wrong, when JJ struck out to end the Yankees' half of the inning.

Wow, Derek thought glumly as he ran back out to short. *That happened fast.*

He forced himself to shake free of his troubles and concentrate with every fiber of his being. He'd have to talk to Avery later.

Harry started the second by tossing a lot of off-speed pitches to the Reds. They hit the ball but didn't make any solid contact. Even though they put two men on base with walks, they didn't score, and the game stayed 2–0.

With Avery batting seventh and leading off the top of the third, Derek had no chance to talk to her. But he noticed she still had that pained look on her face, and she kept wincing every once in a while.

She seemed determined, all right—but it didn't help her any. She struck out on three straight fastballs.

"AAARRRRGH!" she roared, smacking her bat on the ground and yanking off her helmet before stomping back to the bench. She plunked herself down at the far end, away from the rest of the team.

Vijay followed with an infield single—the team's first hit! "Let's go, Yankees!" he shouted, putting his hands over his head and clapping as he stood on first.

Elliott grounded out, sending Vijay to second. Then Mason walked, and Derek came to the plate with two runners on.

Vijay took a big lead off second on the pitch—and Derek saw the shortstop try to sneak in behind him for a pickoff play!

"Get back, Vij!" Derek shouted, just as the catcher fired a bullet to second. Vijay dived back in—and was safe by a whisker.

"Good read, Derek!" Coach K called out to him. "That's heads up! Nice job, Vijay!"

Derek smiled, happy that Vijay had gotten called out for doing something good. But it wouldn't mean much unless Derek drove in the runners in front of him!

The shortstop had backed off from the second base area now and was playing Derek to pull. That left a hole up the middle. Derek planned to put one right through the empty spot. He waited until he saw a high, outside fastball, then swung—

The pitcher dived for cover, and the shortstop and second baseman had no chance, as the ball ripped right up the middle into center field! Vijay, not the fastest kid on the team by any means, still scored—and on the throw, Mason went to third, and Derek wound up on second base!

Now the score was 2–1, and the Yanks had a great chance to take the lead with their home-run leader at the plate. But Pete, too eager to be the hero, swung at a pitch over his head, and popped out to first to dash their hopes.

It wasn't just Pete, Derek knew. A lot of the Yankees were playing tense today. Not Vijay, that was for sure. But everybody else was unusually quiet. They'd come to life when Derek had driven in that run. But now that the rally had been squashed, everything felt flat again.

Harry kept things close, shutting the door on Reds rallies in the third and fourth. In between, the Yankees came close, loading the bases on two hit batters and a walk, but two strikeouts and a groundout finished off the rally. Derek groaned in frustration with each out, and he wasn't the only one.

Now the Yankees were down to their last six outs. One run wasn't much to make up, for sure. But time was running out, not only for the game but for their season!

He could feel the pressure rising, and so could the rest of them. Only Vijay seemed immune, telling everybody they were going to pull this one out of the fire. "Just like we did already. Four times this season, we came from behind to win!"

He'd make a great cheerleader, thought Derek, starting to smile himself—until he caught a glimpse of Avery, sitting at the end of the bench.

She *was* wincing. He *hadn't* imagined it—and holding her stomach too. He made his way down the bench to her, stepping around his other teammates to get there. "You okay?" he asked.

"Been better."

Well, at least she hadn't blown him off. "Do you need a doctor or something?"

She looked at him as if he were from Mars. "Are you for real? We've got a game to win!"

"Right." Okay, so she didn't want to go into it now. Fair enough.

"Okay, then."

"Jeter!" Coach called out to him. "Let's go! You're on deck."

Mason led off the fifth with a walk. Derek doubled him over to third, hitting the first pitch down the right field line. Once again, the Yanks were threatening!

Pete hit a line drive right to the shortstop, who grabbed it, then fired to second. Derek narrowly escaped being doubled off the bag, diving back in just in time. One out.

Harry swung wildly at two bad pitches. Derek winced, wishing Harry would calm himself down. He looked tight as a drum. The next pitch was right over the plate, but Harry watched it go by for strike three. *Two outs.*

Ryan walked to load the bases.

"I'm on deck," Avery said, getting up and pushing past Derek, wincing once again.

"Go get 'em!" he called after her, but she didn't react.

Derek blew out a breath. He sure hoped there was nothing seriously wrong with her. It was all up to JJ now. All he had to do was make solid contact and hit the ball hard someplace—*anyplace*!

He hit it hard, all right. But it was right at the center fielder, who put it away for the third out, leaving three Yankees base runners stranded for the second inning in a row!

A huge groan went up from the entire Yankees bench. Another golden opportunity, maybe their last, had been snuffed out, just like that.

As Avery tossed away the bat she'd been holding, Coach K came up to her. "Mullins," he said, handing her the ball, "you're pitching. Get out there and warm up."

Avery nodded, tensed her jaw, and pounded the ball into her mitt as she ran out to the mound, all fire and determination.

Nobody was immune from nerves, though—not at this point. The Yankees had only three outs left! They had to hold the Reds here, just to give themselves a fighting chance!

Standing at short, Derek could tell right away that Avery was in a zone. She never took her eyes off the catcher as she wound up and threw.

"Strike one!"

Avery hadn't even pitched for the Yankees until halfway through the season. In fact, she'd mostly ridden the bench. It was only after Derek and Vijay had talked her up to Coach Stafford that he'd given her a try at second base in a high-pressure situation. She'd come through with flying colors. Later, after Derek had told the coach she could pitch, he'd tried her there, too, and she'd come through again.

On the next pitch the hitter smacked a grounder Derek's way. He fielded it cleanly and fired to Ryan at first. *One out.*

The next hitter clobbered one to center. But Mason, with his speed, caught up to it and made a really clutch grab.

Derek saw Avery breathe a sigh of relief. Mason's great play must have psyched her up even further, because she put the next hitter away on three perfect pitches—a fastball sandwiched between two wicked changeups.

"All you, Mullins!" Coach K yelled, and the rest of the Yankees cheered as well. Avery didn't acknowledge any of it. She didn't even smile. She just dropped her mitt onto the bench, grabbed a bat, and walked straight to the batter's box.

"Go, Avery!" Derek yelled. "Let's get this rally started!"

She let a fastball go by for a strike. The next pitch was low—but the umpire called it a strike anyway.

"No way!" Avery groaned.

"Play ball!" the ump replied. "Let's go!"

Avery shook her head and dug in. Derek hoped she wouldn't let the ump's bad call get to her. But she did.

The next pitch was outside, but Avery swung anyway, not willing to risk having the ump get it wrong again. The ball ticked off the end of her bat, and the soft liner landed right in the third baseman's glove. Avery groaned.

It's not over yet, Derek told himself. They still had two outs left. Miles came to the plate, hitting for Vijay, who he'd replaced the inning before. He came through, hitting a long fly—but it was run down by the left fielder for the second out.

And now, with only one out left to save their season, it was Norman coming up. Norman, of all people! He rarely played more than two innings in a game, and most of the time he was more interested in goofing around than playing serious ball.

Derek had his heart in his throat, along with the rest of the Yankees. But Norman fooled them all. Baseball, that weirdest of games, took another strange turn—just as the Yankees were about to face the final curtain. Norman took a wild swing at a pitch up in his eyes and hit one straight into the hard ground in front of the plate.

The ball bounced high into the air between home plate and the mound. Norman took a second to look for the ball, which he'd lost sight of. Then, realizing he had a chance, he took off for all he was worth. "RUN! RUUUNNN!" all the Yankees screamed.

"YESSSS!" Derek cried as Norman made it safely to first, just ahead of the throw from the catcher.

Now there was real hope! Mason was a fast, smart player who made contact most of the time.

"Just a ground ball . . . a stupid little grounder," Derek

pleaded under his breath. Half the time, Mason could turn a slow dribbler into a hit.

He did much better than that, though. He hit one down the line that got past the first baseman for a clean double, sending Norman to third!

Derek came to the plate for his biggest at bat of the season. He was the Yankees' last hope. All they needed was a single. . . .

Derek let the count go to 2–1, on three straight fastballs. Something told him the next pitch was going to be off-speed. *Wait on it,* he told himself. *Don't try to do too much.*

Sure enough, it was a curveball. He waited an extra split second, then slapped one over the first baseman's head and into right field. As the ball bounced down the line, Derek raced around first and slid safely into second. Ahead of him, the tying and go-ahead runs scored! 3–2, Yanks!

Derek popped up, ripped off his helmet, and shouted in triumph, *"LET'S GO!"*

But Pete tried to kill the ball again and wound up popping to second to end the Yankees half of the inning. He kicked the dirt, mad at himself for blowing his big chance to put the game away.

Derek was glad he hadn't taken a walk and left it to Pete to drive in those runs! He ran to the bench to grab his mitt, then headed out to short.

Avery was already back on the mound, raring to close things out and seal the victory. Derek could feel waves of energy radiating from her.

Her first pitch sailed two feet over the hitter's head! A gasp went up from the crowd. Her next pitch, a riding fastball, hit him on the elbow.

"OWW!" the kid yelled.

"Take your base!" cried the ump.

The hitter glared at Avery as he walked slowly to first, rubbing the sore spot. She held both arms out and said, "*What?* You think I hit you on purpose?"

He stopped, looking as if he wanted to charge the mound but was thinking twice about it because she was a girl.

"KYLE!" the first-base coach shouted to him. "Knock it off! We've got a game to win—let's go!"

Kyle gave Avery one last poisonous look, then continued on his way, still rubbing his elbow.

Derek saw that Avery was shaken by what had happened. She walked the next batter on four pitches. Then she doubled over, grabbing her stomach.

Coach K jogged quickly out to the mound. "You okay, kid?" he asked, crouching down next to her. Derek, ten feet away, could see that she wasn't.

"I'm fine," she insisted, waving Coach K away. "I'll be fine. I just need a minute to get myself together, that's all."

Coach K looked at her for a long moment, as if he didn't know whether to believe her. Then he got up and clapped her on the shoulder. "Okay, then. Go get 'em, kid."

Avery blew out a few long breaths, trying to calm herself down. The Reds' cleanup hitter was up, waggling his bat, practically salivating, daring her to throw one over the plate.

Her first pitch was a fastball, and he clobbered it all the way to kingdom come—luckily, it landed just foul.

Derek realized he'd been holding his breath—and he knew he wasn't the only one.

That was the last fastball Avery threw him. Two wicked changeups later, he'd struck out, and was slinking his way back to the bench.

Now it was the Reds who were getting antsy and playing tense, Derek noticed.

Avery struck the next batter out too—on three straight changeups, each one slower than the last.

Miles, who'd come in as catcher for JJ in the fifth, threw the ball back to the mound. Avery caught it, then turned toward the outfield as if to rub up the ball. Only Derek could see that she was wincing again.

He jogged in toward her. "Hey," he said. "Just one more out, Ave. You got this?"

"Got it," she said, looking away, still rubbing up the ball.

"Listen," he told her. "This guy at the plate? Stick your tongue out at him before the pitch."

"What?" That got her attention. She was looking at him now—like he was crazy.

"He's thinking changeup now, but you want to throw it anyway. So you've got to get him mad—make him jump too early and swing too hard."

She grinned—sort of. Just a little upward curl at one corner of her mouth. But Derek knew he'd hit the mark. She wouldn't be worried, now that she had a trick up her sleeve.

Derek couldn't see her stick her tongue out, but he saw the hitter react. He stood up straight, frowning, then had to rush back into hitting position to swing.

"Strike one!" called the ump.

The hitter was mad now. Derek could almost see the steam rising from his head! *Now go with the changeup,* he silently begged Avery.

The changeup fooled the hitter so badly that he almost corkscrewed himself into the ground. He was trying to beat the ball into powder, but he caught nothing but air.

"Strike two!"

One more time now. . . . One more . . .

Avery wound up and fired with all her might—or at least that's how it looked. The hitter bought the fake-out totally, and once again swung hard enough to start a tornado. But it was another changeup, and it did the trick!

"Stee-rike three!" the ump yelled.

Ball game!

Avery fell to her knees and screamed in triumph. Everyone rushed to the mound to celebrate. *They'd done it!* The Yankees had lived to play another day!

Everyone started hugging. When Derek got to Avery, she was all smiles, just like the rest of them.

"That tongue idea was awesome!" she told him as they hugged. "Thanks."

"You're welcome," Derek said. "Got to pull out all the stops, right?"

"For sure," she agreed. "Well . . . see you."

"Yup. See you."

Derek went on to hug Vijay, Pete, and all the others. As he did, he noticed Avery and her mom standing side by side near the dugout. Her mom had a hand on Avery's shoulder and was leaning in, asking her something.

Avery just looked down at the ground and shook her head. And then the two of them hugged.

Her mom looked worried. And that made Derek worry.

Was something wrong with Avery? *Really* wrong?

Chapter Seven

CONFIDENCE AND DOUBT

"We won! We won!" Sharlee leapt into Derek's arms as soon as he walked through the front door. "I told you we would! Didn't I? Didn't I say?"

"You did! That's great, Sharlee. What was the score?"

"10–3! And I hit a home run and a suicide fly!"

"*Sacrifice* fly," said Mr. Jeter, coming in from the kitchen with a spatula in one hand and an oven mitt on the other. "Suicide is a kind of squeeze bunt."

"Huh?" Sharlee let go of Derek, looking confused.

"Bunting. They don't let you do it till you're older," Derek explained.

"Anyway, I drove in three runs!" she crowed. "Didn't I, Daddy?"

"Yes indeed," said Mr. Jeter. "Made a nice play at second

base too." He turned to Derek. "I can see by your face that the Yankees won too. Congratulations."

"Thanks," Derek said, flashing a broad grin. "Am I that obvious?"

His dad laughed. "I've know you a long time," he said. "You can't fool your father."

"3–2," Derek said. "We were behind the whole way too!"

"Awesome," said his dad.

"Yeah, awesome!" Sharlee agreed.

"High-five?" Derek offered. When she jumped up to slap his palm, he yelped. "Ow! Hey, don't kill me!" He shook off the pretend pain in his hand, making a tortured face. Sharlee dissolved in giggles.

"Our next game is Saturday!" she told Derek. "Can you come this time at least?"

"What time?" he asked.

"I don't know. Daddy?"

"Nine o'clock," said Mr. Jeter.

"Dang," said Derek. "My game's at nine too."

"So you're not even coming to my game? *Again?*"

"You'll have to win again, so I can come to the next one," Derek said.

"Oh, don't worry—we will," Sharlee assured him. "Right, Daddy?"

A timer dinged in the kitchen. "Excuse me," said Mr. Jeter. "Dinner in five. Derek, table needs setting. Sharlee, make sure you wash up first."

As Derek set the table, he thought about Sharlee's

blissful sense of certainty. He himself was usually just as confident—but not lately, somehow.

And why not? His current coaches might not have been as good as his dad, but they'd done well enough to get the team this far, hadn't they? And as for school, Derek always got good grades—it wasn't like he was in danger of failing or anything.

But something about this past week had shaken his faith in himself. He wasn't used to walking around tense all the time.

"Hey, how'd you guys do yesterday?" Dave asked Derek when they saw each other the next morning outside school. "I can tell you won just by looking at you."

Derek laughed. "Yeah, we came from behind in our last at bat to win, 3–2."

"And I'll bet you were right in the middle of it all too."

"I knocked two runs in with a double," Derek admitted. "It was a great game. You guys ready for Saturday?"

"You bet," Dave said. "We play the Marlins. We're both 6–2 on the season, but they beat us last time, so they're the home team."

"Well, good luck."

"You guys too—you're going to need it. Man, those Giants kicked our butts when we played them."

"Ours too. But hey, you never know. Every game is different—that's why they play 'em, right?"

"Hey, if you guys win, and we do too . . ."

"That's right," Derek said with a grin. "Us versus you guys, winner take all! Let's hope it happens, right?"

"It would be a dream matchup! Tigers–Yankees?"

Suddenly a familiar voice sounded from behind Derek's shoulder. "*Ooooo!* Are we talking *sports* here?"

Derek pivoted to see Gary standing there with his arms crossed over his chest and a big, fat smirk on his face. "Don't tell me you're thinking about *baseball*, Jeter—not when finals start on Monday!"

"I'd better get going," Dave told Derek.

"Can you come out to the Hill tomorrow after school?"

"Uh, not today," Dave said. "My team's got practice. See you, Gary." He waved and went off to his class.

Derek stared after him, feeling jealous. His coaches should have called a practice too. He knew if his dad had been the coach, he would have had one for sure.

Gary and Derek headed for Ms. Terrapin's room. "Do you have to butt into every conversation?" Derek asked him.

"Only the unbearably stupid ones. But honestly, Jeter— how do you expect to beat me next week if your mind is on distractions like baseball? I mean, *baseball*, of all things! Possibly the stupidest of all sports!"

"Okay, Gar, that's enough. We'll talk when you're wearing that chicken suit."

"Oh!" Gary exploded in laughter. "That's a good one!

Well, Jeter, just for that, I'm putting the whammy on you."

Putting out his arms toward Derek and wiggling his fingers as if to cast a spell, he said, "*Abbada-babbada boom!* There. You're cooked." He wiped his hands together, as if to get something nasty off them.

Then he had another idea. "Oh, and here's another, for your big baseball game. *Abbada-babbada LOSE*!"

Derek shook his head, trying not to let Gary's antics get to him. He remembered something his dad had once said: "When somebody is spoiling for a fight with you, sometimes it's better to just walk away. It takes a real grown-up to do that."

So Derek turned away and headed into the classroom, leaving Gary laughing in the hallway behind him. But it was harder to leave his taunting words behind.

As he sat there during finals review, Derek couldn't keep his mind on work. His thoughts kept drifting back to Gary. In particular, those whammies he'd tossed Derek's way.

Derek wasn't usually superstitious. But something about that smirk on Gary's face when he'd laid the whammies on him . . .

Derek felt a shiver go down his spine. *What if Gary's jinxes really work?*

"Come on, Vij. . . . We need to get back to work! It's almost time for you to head home."

"Sorry, Derek. Where were we?"

The two boys were sitting side by side at Derek's desk. Textbooks lay open between them, along with sample pages of standardized tests that Ms. Terrapin had given them for practice at home.

"It's almost six already," Derek said, glancing at the alarm clock on his bedside table. "We've only got, like, ten more minutes. Did we make any headway at all today?"

"A little," Vijay said weakly.

The two boys had spent more time talking about Dave moving away than about their upcoming finals.

"I still can't believe it," Vijay had said shortly after they'd sat down to study together. "It's like he just moved here, and now he's going?"

"It's been two years," Derek had replied. "Dave says it's the second longest time his family has lived in one place. Can you imagine?"

"It's not going to be the same without him," Vijay had said sadly. He'd seemed really upset—as upset as Derek. And Vijay *never* got upset!

"I never thought about him leaving," Derek had said, "and then one day, just like that—*bam*!"

They'd gone on and on about Dave. Then, after they'd finally gotten back to studying, Derek had kept flashing back to the image of Avery doubled over, holding her stomach. If she'd gone to Saint Augustine, like them, he would at least have known if she'd stayed home from school today.

When Vijay had asked what was distracting him, Derek had told him what he'd seen.

"She is under a lot of pressure, I think," Vijay had said, nodding. "More than the rest of us."

So they'd talked a little about her, wondering whether she'd be okay for their next game on Saturday. They agreed it would be tough to win without her.

They'd gotten back to work one more time, but that had lasted only about twenty minutes, and then they were talking about Dave again. They agreed to tag-team writing Dave letters, so he got one every week. That solution helped Derek felt a little better about things. But now their study time was almost up—and nearly all wasted!

"Well," Vijay said now, shrugging, "what can we do in ten minutes to make up for lost time? Is there some big knot we can untie?"

Derek held up the practice sheets for the standardized tests. "I'm a little spooked about these, to tell you the truth."

"Those?" Vijay sounded surprised. "Those are easy! Just like the ones they gave us in fourth grade. No problem for a smart kid like you."

"I don't know. . . . I kind of got messed up last time. The teacher said to make sure we filled in the circles completely."

"So?"

"So, I spent so much time filling them in, and sharpening my pencil, which kept breaking from all the pressure I was putting on it . . ."

"I see where you're going here."

". . . that I didn't even finish the test! There were, like, three whole pages of questions left!"

"You still scored pretty high, as I remember," Vijay said.

"Not as high as I should have."

"So, quickly, before time is up—do you want to know a trick I taught myself to finish fast?"

"Seriously?" Derek asked, his eyes widening.

"Here's how you do it," Vijay said, rubbing his hands together as he warmed to his subject. "First time through, you only tackle the questions you know the answers to. Any doubts, leave it for now and come back to it later, in round two."

"And round three?"

"Is for the ones you have no clue about. And make sure you at least answer all of those, too—even if you're wrong. At least that way you have a chance of getting it right!"

"You taught yourself that trick?"

"Nooo," Vijay said with a grin. "My parents knew these tests were coming, and they wanted me to score my highest, so they signed me up for a prep course last year."

Derek smiled, and clapped Vijay on the shoulder. "Man, you are the best. I'm going to put those tricks to good use."

"Look out, Gary Parnell!" Vijay said, and they both cracked up as they high-fived.

Derek was feeling much better, at least for the moment. Even if he lost Dave, he still had a best friend in Vijay—and there was no better friend in the world for a guy to have.

Chapter Eight

AVERY'S QUEST

Avery seemed pretty much fine, Derek observed, as they threw the ball around what passed for the infield on Jeter's Hill. She seemed, if not relaxed and happy, at least fairly normal. She wasn't clutching her stomach and wincing. She didn't even look that stressed—in spite of the fact that they had a huge game coming up the next morning.

Derek guessed that she needed to get away from the pressures she lived with most of the time. He also sensed that today might be his best chance to sound her out, and find out what was really bugging her.

The pickup game got started. At one point Avery fielded a grounder with a man on first, and flipped to Derek to start the double play—but she tossed it to the wrong side of the bag, making it impossible for him to get off a strong throw to first.

"Hey," he told her. "You wanna hang around after and practice a few of those, so we get it right if it happens tomorrow?"

"Sure!" she said without hesitation.

Derek wasn't surprised she'd taken him up on his offer. Avery never turned down an opportunity to improve her game.

Vijay was the last of the others to leave. "I have to get home and heat up dinner," he told Derek and Avery. "My parents get home from work at six thirty."

Vijay's parents worked at the hospital, and sometimes didn't get home until late, so heating up dinner was pretty routine at the Patel house.

"Cool," said Avery. As Vijay walked away, she turned to Derek. "So . . . practice?"

"Uh, yeah. Listen . . . could I just ask you—"

"I thought you wanted to run double-play drills," she said, hands on her hips.

"Yeah, right—but . . . Look, you're probably going to get mad at me, but I've just got to ask. Is there something going on with you lately? I mean, are you *okay*? You're not sick or something?"

"Do we have to talk about this?"

"Yes. Be mad at me if you want, but at least let me know what's going on. I mean, I thought we were friends."

"We are," she said. Then, with a sigh, she continued, "Okay, I'll admit it. The pressure's been getting to me lately. I guess when I got into all this, I figured I could take whatever abuse I got, and still go on. You know, because of my brother and all."

"Yeah? And?"

"I guess I didn't figure in the *other* kind of pressure."

"As in winning?"

"Kind of. I mean, I was just going to *play* in his honor, and do him proud. But once we got in sight of the playoffs, I guess I just moved the goalposts. It's . . . the pressure just builds and builds and builds. And now . . ."

"I hear you. But you know, you've done great. You're *doing* great!"

"Thanks. But it's really starting to get to me. Every time I blow it out there, I want to kick myself."

"Well, don't do *that*!" Derek said, trying to inject a little levity. She didn't even crack a smile.

"In fact, I was thinking that I might not sign up again next year."

"What?"

Avery shrugged. "You know, just go back to soccer, maybe lacrosse or even volleyball."

Derek looked at her like he'd never seen her before. Avery was sure full of surprises!

"My mom was the same way," she went on. "You know, she was playing in the boys' leagues a long time ago, when girls were first allowed by law. It was really, really tough on her. Tougher than on me, even."

Derek wished he could help her somehow. He decided to talk to his mom and dad about it. He was pretty sure they'd have some good ideas.

"Listen," he said. "It's getting late. Why don't I just walk you home, and we can work the DP again before the game tomorrow?"

"Okay."

As they walked, Derek couldn't help but think about what a cost she'd paid all season long. To become the kind of ballplayer she was—playing a new sport for the first time, as the only girl in the whole league, and doing it to honor your late brother? Not so easy.

"You know," he told her, "I've kind of been feeling the pressure too."

"Yeah?"

"Maybe not like you, but for sure. I'm having trouble studying for finals—"

"Hah! Me too!" At last she cracked a smile.

"Yeah, but you didn't make a bet with someone where the guy with the lower score has to wear a chicken suit the last day of school!"

"You did *not*!"

Derek nodded sadly.

"No way! Oh, poor Derek—why did you go and do that?"

"Because I'm a dummy. But no, seriously, I'm going to

hang that chicken suit on that kid. Some way, somehow . . ."

"You think?"

"Hey, I've got Vijay helping me—how can I lose?"

Sharlee had been acting mysteriously the whole evening. All through dinner she kept exchanging sneak peeks with her mom and giggling, while looking at Derek. He suspected it had something to do with his upcoming birthday, and whatever surprise the two of them were hatching for him.

After helping wash and dry the dinner dishes, Derek left the two plotters to their own devices, and went to find his dad.

Mr. Jeter was at the desk in his home office, grading his students' papers. He worked as a college professor at Western Michigan University.

"Derek?"

"Hi, Dad. Could I, um, could I talk to you about something?"

His dad swiveled his chair around. "Sure! Have a seat, Son. What's on your mind?"

"It's about Avery."

"Avery?" Mr. Jeter looked surprised.

"I just don't know what to do, and I thought you might be able to help." Derek filled his dad in on everything he'd noticed about Avery over the past three weeks.

"Hmmm," Mr. Jeter said when Derek had finished.

"Sounds like she's making herself sick over it."

"Exactly!"

"She might not be in the mood to listen, no matter what good advice you might have for her, Derek. You know, in our house, we are very competitive and we always play to win. We take the field expecting it, and we're not happy when we lose. But one thing you *can't* say about us is that we don't have fun playing the game. If we didn't, what would be the point of the whole thing?"

"Huh," Derek said, nodding slowly.

"If Avery realized that teams lose championships much more than they win them, she might feel differently, maybe go a little easier on herself. Remember, players who get a hit one third of the time in their careers go to the Hall of Fame."

"Wow. I never thought of it like that." Derek had hit way better than .333 for his Little League career. He felt a sudden flush of pride go through him.

"You know, Derek, you seem pretty wound up yourself lately," his dad said, taking him by surprise. "Maybe you should consider some of this stuff too."

"I'm fine, Dad. It's Avery I'm worried about."

"Well, then, tell *Avery* to go out there and just have fun. Tell her that her brother would be proud of her, no matter what happens. Win or lose."

Derek nodded. He knew his dad was right.

Mr. Jeter continued, "I seem to recall that your teams

haven't won championships every time. But you're still crazy about baseball."

"That's for sure," Derek said, grinning.

"And you've still got big dreams for yourself, right?"

"Totally!"

"You know, I had big baseball dreams, just like you."

"I know, Dad."

"I didn't get there in the end, but maybe you will, Derek. Anyway, I wouldn't have traded that time for anything. And I *enjoyed every minute*."

"Thanks, Dad," Derek said, getting up and giving him a hug. "Thanks for that."

"Remember, it's fine to be serious about things. It's fine to care with all your heart. But you've got to be able to enjoy the ride, win or lose. Always go out to do the best you can and have fun along the way."

Chapter Nine

GIANT KILLERS?

Swinging a pair of bats to limber up, Derek looked into the stands. There was his mom, talking to Vijay's parents. The Patels had Saturday off for a change and seemed excited and happy to be there.

And there was Avery's mom, standing in the back row of the bleachers, next to the older boys who served with her as Avery's cheering section. Avery's mom had been at almost every game, but Derek had never really met her, except to shake hands once.

But one thing about her—she was *into* it. Right now she stood facing Avery, her hands on Avery's shoulders as the two of them leaned their heads in together. It looked to Derek like a very private, very intense pep talk. When it was over, Avery's mom worked her daughter's shoulders, then clapped them one last time. Avery nodded, blowing off big breaths like they were clouds of tension.

Derek wondered if Avery's mom was as stressed out as her daughter was.

"Yanks, huddle up!" Coach K called out. Derek joined the rest of the team as they gathered around for their pregame pep talk.

"Okay, guys," said Coach Stafford. "This is our biggest game yet."

"Yeah! Yeah!" The Yanks were already psyched to the max. Derek joined in, raising both bats in the air.

"Now, these guys are really good," the coach went on. "You remember them from the regular season. They're undefeated for a reason. So . . . I don't want you to be too disappointed if we don't win today."

Huh? Derek couldn't believe his ears! Was their coach really trying to prepare them to *lose*?

"I want you to remember, guys—and girl," Coach Stafford added with a nod to Avery, "we've already had a great, great season. Right?"

There was a weak echo from a few of the kids, but Derek could tell they were already getting bummed out by their coach's tone. Wasn't this supposed to be a chance to rev them up? Why was he trying to let them down easy—*in advance?*

Now more than ever, Derek wished it were his dad and

Chase who were leading them into battle. But Derek also knew that you go to war with the coaches you have, not the ones you *wish* you had.

"I want you all to go out there today and just have fun," Coach Stafford finished. "Have a blast—and may the best team win. Hopefully, the ball bounces our way, right?"

He clapped his hands twice, but nobody else joined in. "Okay, let's do our cheer! Here we go—hands in." They piled their mitts on top of one another and yelled, "Goooo, Yanks!" Then they broke off to play ball.

Derek glanced over at Avery. She looked as upset as he felt.

Well, of course! Sure, you had to enjoy every moment. But Derek only knew one way to compete—full-out. And he knew that went double for Avery. "Hey," he said, trying to get her to smile. "Just like we do it on the Hill, right? Nice and loose."

Avery almost smiled, but not quite. At the last minute she turned away, to be alone again for one final moment with her private thoughts.

She and Derek had both shown up early today, as planned, to practice their double-play pivots and footwork. Vijay had come along, to help them out by playing first base.

After half an hour of drilling, their timing in the infield felt almost automatic. Derek only hoped it would help during the game.

As the playoff team with the worse regular-season

record, the Yanks were the visitors today. Derek grabbed his bat and went to the on-deck circle, while Mason dug in at home plate.

Derek knew that the Giants had been routing opponents all season. They'd scored a ton of runs, and they had two shut-down pitchers—which was two more than most teams in the league.

It was going to take the Yankees' best effort to win this game. And more—it was going to take some luck and creativity to keep up with the mighty Giants. The Yankees were going to have to cash in on any breaks they got.

And they got one right away! Mason reached for a low outside pitch and sent a looping fly to short left. It fell just out of reach of the shortstop and third baseman, who nearly collided in the process.

Derek picked up some dirt from the ground and rubbed it between his palms, in case they were sweaty. With this pitcher you had to swing your hardest just to keep up with his fastballs, and you didn't want the bat slipping in your hands.

Looking out at the fielders, Derek saw that they were playing him to pull. He waited for an outside fastball, got one on a 1–1 count, and slapped it through the hole on the right side of the infield. It just missed Mason—which was another lucky break, because he would have been called out if the ball had hit him. Instead he made it all the way to third, as the throw came in to second base.

Pete was up next. He stared at a strike right over the middle. Then another. Derek knew that the pitcher would likely get Pete to swing at a bad pitch for the strikeout. If it got away from the catcher, Derek would be on his way to second.

But the next pitch was in the dirt. It bounced off the catcher's chest pad—not very far, but Derek was off in an instant. The catcher panicked and threw to second—forgetting that there was also a runner on third!

The throw was perfect, and just in time to nail Derek for the out—but the run scored without a throw to home plate, and suddenly the Yankees were in the lead, 1–0!

Pete swung at the next pitch, and hit a fly to left for the second out.

That brought Harry to the plate. He was not as powerful as Pete but was better at making contact because he didn't try to hit every ball out of the park. That made him a good matchup against the Giants' starter. As hard as he threw, you only had to meet the ball and it would go a long way.

Easier said than done. But on the second pitch, Harry connected, hitting a screaming liner that sent the center fielder way, way back!

Derek was sure it was going to be over the center fielder's head, but the kid ran it down for the third out. "Rats!" Derek shouted, kicking the dirt in frustration. *So close!*

The Yanks had succeeded at step one—getting a lead.

Now it was the Giants' turn to show what they could do with a bat. They had come in superconfident, but now they would have to come from behind, against a team they *just might* have underestimated.

Good, thought Derek. If the Yanks could get the Giants a little spooked, maybe they would start to play tight, instead of loose and free.

The leadoff man hit a hard line drive to Avery at second. With a well-timed leap, she snagged it, and came down screaming, "YAAAH!" The other Yanks let out a cheer as she tossed it back to the mound with a loud "LET'S GO!"

No way would Pete have made that play if he were at second, Derek thought. It had been Pete's position at the start of the season, before Avery had replaced him. Now Pete was starting at third—a much better fit for a guy his size, who wasn't as athletic or mobile as Avery.

Derek took a few steps in toward Harry on the mound. "Hey," Derek called, motioning for Harry to come closer. "Listen," he said in a low voice, "they're dying to hit dingers. Try playing with 'em a little—let 'em get *themselves* out, huh?"

Harry grinned and nodded. "Sure thing," he said. "Why not?"

The next two hitters swung hard enough to hit it all the way to Detroit, but they only succeeded in grounding out on Harry's changeups.

The Yanks came back up to bat, still ahead by one run.

But there was a long, long way to go. And their hitters weren't even close to solving the Giants' starter. He struck out Ryan, and after a walk to Avery, he fanned JJ and Tre' to set the Yankees down.

In the bottom of the inning, the Giants worked a walk with one out. The next batter smashed one just to Derek's right. He gobbled the ball up and fired to Avery, covering second. She took the throw in stride, pivoted as if it were second nature, and fired to first for the easy double play!

"Just like we practiced!" he told her—and this time she really did smile back.

The Yanks went down on three more strikeouts in the third: Elliott, Vijay, and Mason.

In the bottom of the inning, with runners on first and second and one out, Avery dived to her right to grab a sizzling grounder that had "RBI" written all over it. After snagging it like a sno-cone in the webbing of her mitt, she flicked it straight from her glove to Derek at second. He caught it bare-handed and fired to first, just in time to complete the amazing double play!

End of inning—no runs scored! All their extra work had already paid off big-time!

So far the Yankees' luck was holding up. But it was hanging by a very slender one-run thread, especially against the Giants—the best-hitting team in the league by far.

Derek led off the top of the fourth, determined to get

something started. He knew the Yanks would need more than one run to win the game. He took one strike, watched two straight balls go by, and then fouled off a fastball for strike two.

Protect . . . protect, he told himself. No way did he want to get called out on strikes to lead off an inning!

He fouled off another fastball, then another and another. The pitcher tried a changeup, but it missed for ball three.

Would he throw another changeup? Derek guessed not. He geared up for the fastball and fouled off yet another. Two more foul balls later, and the pitcher finally gave in and tried another changeup.

"Ball four!" cried the ump.

Derek trotted down to first, looking at his teammates and clapping his hands. "Let's go!" he called, pointing a finger at them to urge them on.

Pete grounded out on the first pitch, overanxious, as he often was. Derek made it to second, though, so it was a productive out at least.

Harry stepped to the plate. When the pitcher threw him an 0–2 changeup, it was inside, and nearly hit him. The ball got away from the catcher, and Derek raced to third!

"Come on, Harry!" he called, cupping his hands to his mouth to make a megaphone.

Harry dug in. The next pitch was a fastball, but Harry was ready. He sent a long fly to left, where the Giants' fielder was parked under it.

As soon as the Giants player caught the ball, Derek took off for home. The throw came in way too late. 2–0, Yankees! And they'd gotten the second run without even getting a hit!

Ryan struck out to end the Yankees' half of the inning, but now, at least, the Yanks had a bit of a cushion. If their pitching held up, they would pull off the biggest upset of the entire season!

Harry had already thrown a lot of pitches in the first three innings. Now it started to show. He walked the first two men he faced, wasting thirteen pitches in the process. Derek knew the coach would have to make a pitching change soon, because Harry was clearly running out of bullets *and* gas.

Coach K called time and jogged out to the mound. Derek walked closer to hear the conversation. "You okay, Hicks?"

"I'm good," Harry answered, looking down at the ground. He sure didn't *seem* good, Derek observed.

"All right, go get 'em," Coach K said with a pat on Harry's shoulder, and he headed back to the bench.

Harry struck out the next batter by fooling him on a series of pitches. But the third strike got away from Miles, who'd come in to replace JJ behind the plate. Although he tagged the hitter out, both runners advanced without a throw, and now it was second and third with one out.

That wound up hurting the Yankees on the very next

pitch. The hitter lofted a fly ball to Vijay, in right. He caught it for the second out, but the runner scored from third easily, to make it a 2–1 game. Meanwhile, the runner at second advanced to third.

Derek concentrated as hard as he could, just hoping that Harry would find some magic to get them out of this inning with only the one run.

But the magic they needed turned out to be in Derek's glove. The batter hit a pop fly to shallow left. It wasn't deep enough for Tre' to come in from left and catch it. It wasn't hit high enough for Pete to get there from third.

It was up to him, and Derek was already running full tilt, looking back over his shoulder as he went, trying to keep the ball in his sights. He heard everyone screaming as he leapt forward, his arm outstretched to the limit. The ball hit the webbing, then shook loose and flew back into the air!

Derek rolled over twice, and saw the ball coming back down just to his left. He reached out—and came down with it!

Three outs! And the Yankees were still in the lead, 2–1!

"Play of the game, Jeter!" Coach K said as Derek's teammates all gathered around to high-five him.

"Let's go!" he told them. "It's not over yet!" And to Avery, who already had a bat in her hands, ready to lead off, Derek said, "Come on, Ave—get us started!"

After switching around to hit righty against the Giants'

lefty reliever, Avery let the first two pitches go by, getting a good look at the reliever's style.

Then, with a 1–1 count, she jumped on a fastball and lined a double to right center! As she reached second, she lifted both arms in the air, then pointed to Derek and the others.

"Way to go!" Derek yelled back at her. "That's it!"

The mood was electric on the Yankees bench, and when JJ worked a walk, the voltage went even higher.

Tre' would normally have been up next. But for the fifth inning, Coach had made his mandatory substitutions. Tre', a much better hitter, had to watch from the bench as Miles struck out.

Elliott was next. He swung weakly at two pitches, then got hit in the arm with a changeup. "Ow!" he yelled, but nevertheless, he was smiling as he jogged down to first.

Now the bases were full of Yankees. Vijay would have been up, but he'd been replaced by Norman, who didn't get that many at bats, and wasn't used to hitting lefty pitching.

Norman ducked out of the way of two pitches that wound up curving in for strikes. Then he whiffed at a fastball way outside to end the Yankees' half of the inning, stranding three runners and dashing the team's hopes.

As Avery came back to the dugout, Derek tried to give her a fist bump for getting that clutch hit, but she ignored him, lost in her own frustration.

Coach K came up to her. "Mullins," he said. "You're pitching the fifth. Get out there and warm up."

Avery had been okay today, until that moment. But as Coach K walked away from her, Derek saw her wince and falter, clutching her stomach again.

"Hey," he said. "What's up with you, anyway? You should be seeing a doctor about that."

"NOT NOW!" she growled at him through gritted teeth. After grabbing a ball from the bench, she slammed it into her mitt and headed off toward the mound, leaving Derek staring after her.

Chapter Ten

FIGHT FOR SURVIVAL

Derek could tell that Avery was in high-tension mode. Her shoulders were high up, almost to her ears, a sure sign she wasn't feeling loose and easy.

But Derek didn't need to see all that to know. Because he *knew* her, and he had some idea of what she was going through inside.

The Giants were watching as she warmed up, making quiet jokes about her, and cracking one another up. *Pretty cocky for a team that's losing,* Derek thought.

But he understood why. The Giants hadn't lost all year. Why shouldn't they expect to win every time they took the field? A one-run deficit? That was not going to faze them. And a girl pitching? They must have thought this was going to be a pushover.

Avery did get the first two strikes on the first hitter. But then he poked a single into right field, and from that moment, the feeding frenzy was on. There were hoots and hollers, and some taunts flung at Avery from the Giants bench.

The next batter smashed a line drive to center. Luckily, it was right at Mason, who flinched, but caught the ball and threw it back in to hold the runner at first.

The Giants bench quieted down, but only for a moment. Avery blew out a relieved breath, then smacked herself angrily on the side of her head with her mitt.

"Hey!" Derek called out to her. "No getting down on yourself, huh? You got this!"

She threw him a hard glance, then got back to business. The catcalls continued, and Derek felt like calling time, going over there, and giving them all a piece of his mind. But he knew he'd better concentrate on doing his job.

On Avery's next pitch the hitter smacked a hard grounder to second, where Harry had taken over when Avery had come in to pitch. Harry fielded the ball cleanly, then threw to Derek at second to start the double play.

But Harry hadn't been there early to take infield practice. His throw sailed wide of the bag, just off the tip of Derek's mitt! Avery, backing up the play smartly, picked up the ball and checked the runner. She then walked back to the mound, muttering under her breath.

She was as mad as she could be, and no wonder, Derek thought. She'd succeeded in getting that grounder, only to have an easy double play messed up behind her. Because she wasn't the one playing second base. And the kid who was playing there hadn't practiced with Derek beforehand. So instead of the inning being over, now it was first and second, with only one out.

Derek called over to Harry. "Don't worry, man—we've got this."

Harry nodded, but didn't look back at him. Clearly he felt bad for messing up at a crucial moment. But at least now he knew his teammates were behind him.

Avery was laser-focused on the Giants' next hitter, who was waggling his bat over his head, like he smelled blood in the water.

Derek could see the sweat trickling down Avery's face. He wanted to tell her to relax and settle down. But after the look she'd just given him and Harry, he hesitated.

He soon wished he hadn't. On the first pitch the hitter sent one deep to left center. It split the outfielders, for a double that scored both runners, and put the Giants ahead for the first time in the game, 3–2!

Coach Stafford was already out of the dugout and headed for the mound. He signaled to Pete to come in from third to pitch. Harry went back to third, his usual position when he wasn't pitching. And Avery was sent back to play second base.

Derek followed her with his gaze. He could tell she was steaming, even though her face was hidden.

Pete started off by plunking the first hitter he faced. For a moment Derek feared that things were going to go from bad to worse. Were the Yankees about to fall apart completely?

Pete ran the count full, then threw one right over the plate. The hitter sent a liner to Derek's left side. Reacting without thinking, he ran for it, and grabbed it in stride for the out.

Then, seeing that the runner on second had strayed too far and slipped trying to get back, Derek kept going, and his foot touched the bag an instant before the runner's.

"OUT!" shouted the ump.

Inning over! Unassisted double play!

Letting out a triumphant shout, Derek ran excitedly back to the bench.

A second ago the season had looked like it was about to go up in flames. If he hadn't made that play, Derek knew, his team would have been behind now by at least two runs.

Instead the deficit was only one. With three outs left, and the top of their order coming up, the Yankees still had a fighting chance!

Derek watched the new Giants pitcher warm up. Yet another hard thrower. Derek could hear the catcher's mitt make a loud pop every time the ball hit it.

Okay, he told himself. *I've got to be ready for the fastball.*

Mason couldn't catch up to it and wound up striking out. Now the Yanks were down to two outs.

And Derek was up.

He took a pitch, hoping to get ahead in the count, but it was a strike. Just watching it go by, Derek knew he was going to have a problem getting onto this kid's fastball. But he also saw that the infielders were playing him deep—*too* deep.

The next pitch was a low fastball. Derek took just a half swing at it—not a bunt, but not a full swing either. The ball bounced slowly to the pitcher's right, forcing him to turn awkwardly out of his follow-through and field the ball, then pivot and throw to first.

He might still have gotten Derek for the out. But his throw was wide to the left. It got by the first baseman, and Derek wound up on second!

Now the Yankees had some life! Derek could feel it, and so could his teammates. They were going wild on the bench, yelling at the top of their lungs for Pete to hit one out of the park.

Pete always wanted to be the big hero with the big hit. Well, this was the perfect time. The pitcher didn't want to walk him, putting the go-ahead run on base. So Pete was going to get a good pitch to swing at.

Expecting a fastball, he started his swing early, and pulled a sharp liner into left, deep enough to score Derek with the tying run!

Pete stood on second, clapping as Derek ran back to the bench. The Giants looked worried now, and the Yankees were making a world of noise. Derek took his high fives, rattled the chain-link fence, and yelled his head off for Harry to keep the rally going.

With the count full, Harry took a huge swing, and hit a soft fly to shallow right center. The right fielder, seeing the big swing, had misjudged it and backed up two steps, before realizing Harry hadn't gotten all of it.

By the time the right fielder realized his mistake, it was too late—he raced back in, just as the center fielder and second baseman arrived at the same spot. The ball fell between them, and Pete wound up on third, with Harry on first!

"WOO-HOO!" The Yankees and their fans were all on their feet, shouting and cheering.

Ryan was up next. His fly to center was the second out, but it was deep enough to score Pete, and the Yankees were back in the lead, 4–3!

The Giants erupted into shouts, blaming the right fielder for messing up. Their coach had to call time and go onto the field to keep a fight from starting between his players!

Derek felt sorry for the kid in right field. It was an easy mistake to make, and most kids wouldn't have done any better, he knew. But he was glad the Giants were upset.

A rattled team is a losing team.

Avery struck out to end the Yankees sixth, and came back to the bench in a rage, shaking the chain-link fence to work off the frustration before grabbing her mitt to get back out in the field.

"We've got 'em where we want 'em," Derek said under his breath, pounding his glove. He glanced over at Avery. She looked right back at him, her eyes ablaze with intensity.

Pete took the mound. He was clearly feeling good about himself, after finally coming through for his team at the key moment. Pete was big and strong, if not a particularly accurate thrower. But the Giants were desperate now. They were trying to get that run back with every swing they took.

Between Pete's wildness and their overeager swings, the mighty Giants had no chance. They went down one, two, three—on two grounders and a weak pop-up!

In the biggest upset of the entire Little League season, the lowly wild-card Yankees had dispatched the undefeated kings of the regular season!

Against all odds, they'd done it. And now they were just one win away from the championship!

Chapter Eleven

DAVE

That night after dinner, the phone rang. "It's for you, Derek," said his mom, handing him the phone. "Dave."

"Hello?" Derek said anxiously. He'd been waiting for Dave's call.

"Guess what? *We won!*" Derek could hear the excitement in his friend's voice.

"Wow! That's great!"

"You know what this means, right?"

"It's us versus you for the big prize! I can't believe it!"

"What were the odds?"

"It's going to be one heck of a game."

"Oh, man . . ."

Derek heard the sudden hesitation in Dave's voice. "What?"

"You sure you're okay about it?"

"Huh? What do you mean?"

"I know how much this means to you," Dave said. "It means a ton to *me*, so I can only imagine . . ." Dave loved all sports, but he knew baseball was Derek's passion. If it had been a golf tournament, the shoe would have been on the other foot.

"Don't worry about it—because you guys are *not* going to win."

Dave let out a relieved laugh. "Okay, we'll see. But *if* we win, and *if* I hit three homers or something—are you still going to write to me?"

Derek was suddenly caught up short. "Of course!" he said. "Are you kidding?"

"Kind of," Dave said. "But . . . well, with the move and everything, I thought maybe—"

"Never! Not on *my* end, at least."

"Mine neither."

"Okay, then."

"Okay," said Dave. "I guess . . . I guess I'll see you at school tomorrow."

"Yeah. Sure. And hey, don't worry—it's going to be a great game. And whatever happens, nothing changes between us."

"Right. Nothing changes." There was a short silence. "Bye, then."

"Bye." Derek hung up, feeling a little rattled. Somehow,

when the playoffs had started, it had seemed like such a long shot that he and Dave would wind up playing each other in the final game.

He wasn't sure how happy he was about it. If Dave was worried it would affect their friendship, should Derek have been worried too?

How would he really feel if the Yankees went down in defeat *because of Dave*? Not great, that was for sure. He guessed it would be better if Dave was the Tigers hero, rather than some other kid. But Derek wasn't sure how he would feel. You never really knew until the moment came.

One thing was certain—between now and Saturday, he and Dave were competitors. One of their teams was going to win the championship.

And one wasn't.

Derek could feel the cold sweat in his armpits. It wasn't like normal sweat—the kind you work up when you're active. This was the sweat of anxiety. Of *fear*.

Glancing over at his rival, Derek saw that Gary was busy filling in answer after answer. He had a relaxed, satisfied smile on his face—the smile of a tiger after eating its prey.

Wait—was Gary actually *humming*?

Looking up at the clock behind Ms. Terrapin's desk, Derek saw that he was now behind in time. He felt a surge of alarm go through him. The cold sweat was now showing through his T-shirt.

Come on, said a little voice in Derek's head. *Math is your best subject!* Derek remembered his dad's advice: "You can't do your best if you're stressed."

It's just a bunch of puzzles to be solved, that's all, Derek told himself. *Puzzles are fun, right?*

He smiled. The voice sounded a lot like Vijay. Derek looked over at his friend. Vijay looked calm, unworried, and totally focused.

Derek tried to get back to work, but Gary's soft humming kept distracting him.

And then, he thought of the chicken suit. He saw himself, surrounded by classmates pointing at him and laughing. Even the little kids were laughing and pointing. He would never live it down.

The image was enough to shock Derek back into action. The jumble of facts in his brain suddenly reorganized itself. Remembering Vijay's advice, he quickly sailed through a raft of easy questions, skipping anything he didn't instantly know the answer to. These weren't the standardized tests, he reasoned, but the same strategy ought to work with any test, right?

Going back to tackle the harder problems, Derek found to his surprise that he really did know most of the answers, especially the multiple-choice items. He finished the second go-round with ten minutes left.

He was just answering the last problem when time ran out. "Pencils down!" Ms. Terrapin said.

Whew. He'd done it—just barely, but Derek felt satisfied that in the end he'd done the best he could. He was pretty confident that studying with Vijay had made a huge difference. More than anything, it had given him the confidence that he could do it.

"Well, Gary," Derek said as they filed out of the classroom, "may the best man win."

Gary snorted. "He already has, Jeter. You just haven't gotten the bad news yet."

Derek laughed, shaking his head. "Messing with my head, huh? Nice. Same old Gary."

"Come on, Jeter—don't pretend you don't do the same."

"Me?"

"Look at you, Mr. Goody Two-shoes. Are you telling me you're not messing with my head just as much? Well, I don't buy your 'innocent' act for a minute."

"I don't know what you're talking about, Gar. I don't play like that. Those kinds of sports really *are* a waste of time."

"Don't kid me, Jeter. This is only round one, and you were struggling in there, I could tell. And math is supposed to be your best subject? Man, you're in deep trouble."

Derek kept his arms close to his sides, so Gary wouldn't see the sweat stains under his arms. "Is that what you think, Gar? Well, good for you. You just keep thinking it."

"Uh-huh. I'm not buying any of this stuff, Jeter—but have it your way."

"Thanks, I'll do that. Better start practicing your clucking, my friend."

Gary stood there watching him go, seeds of doubt sprouting in his suspicious brain. "If you win, I'll know you cheated," he called after Derek.

Derek took one last glance behind him, just to see the look on Gary's face as his supreme confidence began to wobble just a little bit.

Good, thought Derek. *Now at least he knows how it feels.*

When Derek got off the school bus and rounded the corner of his block, he saw the black sedan parked in front of his house.

"Dave! Hi," he called, waving to his friend.

Dave was standing on the sidewalk, waiting for him. "Hi," he said as he and Derek went through their elaborate private handshake.

"I can't hang out today," Derek said apologetically. "I have to study for tomorrow's English final."

"I know. Me too. I . . . I just wanted to talk for a few minutes."

"Okay."

Dave looked down the path, toward the Patels' townhouse. "Can we talk inside?"

"Uh . . . sure." Derek waved to Chase, who was sitting behind the wheel. "Hi."

Chase waved back and smiled. "Good to see you, Derek."

"Come on in." Derek led Dave up the front stairs and inside. "My parents will be glad to see you. It's been a while."

"Dave!" Mr. Jeter said, getting up from the couch and coming over to shake Dave's hand. "How's it going?"

Dave sighed. "Not so great, Mr. Jeter. Derek told you we're moving?"

"He did. I'm very sorry to hear it. We're going to miss you, Dave. Derek most of all."

"Thanks. I'm going to miss you all too."

"Let me go rustle up some snacks for you," Mr. Jeter said, leaving them alone in the living room.

"It feels like months since I've been here," Dave began.

"I know! Half the time it feels like you're already gone. I mean, I know we've all been busy with playoffs and finals and stuff. But you never even come out to the Hill anymore."

"I've been packing up all my stuff." Dave was looking straight down at the floor. "On top of studying and playoffs. You know, when you're feeling cruddy, you don't really feel like hanging out with people. You don't want them to see you like that . . . to remember you like that."

A long silence followed. Mr. Jeter returned with a plate of cookies and two glasses of milk. Then, sensing the heavy atmosphere and realizing the boys needed some space to talk, he went back into the kitchen.

The two boys ate and drank in silence, each waiting for the other to say something. Finally Dave put down his glass and heaved a big sigh. "I don't *want* to go anywhere!" he cried. "I like it *here*!"

"Well . . . you know, maybe Hong Kong will be great," Derek said, trying to console his friend. "I mean, if you have to go, you might as well get excited about it. Right?"

"That's what my parents keep saying. 'You're going to love it there!' I'll believe it when I see it."

Derek could see that Dave was close to tears. Luckily, just then the doorbell rang. "That's Vijay for sure!"

Dave got up, sniffing. "I guess I'll see you . . . whenever."

"Look," Derek said, trying to find something to say. "We'll find some time before you leave, to hang out. After playoffs and finals are over, but before . . . you know."

Dave shrugged. "That only leaves a few days. And it'll be chaos over at my house."

"We'll find the time somehow," Derek insisted. "Maybe even play a round of golf, or at least hit some balls at the range?"

Derek knew that would lift Dave's spirits, and sure enough, it brought out a smile. Dave's dream was to be a pro golfer someday. He enjoyed other sports, but nothing compared to golf.

"That'd be awesome! Let's do it!"

The doorbell rang again, more insistently this time.

"Great," said Derek, opening the door and clapping Dave on the shoulder. "See you then."

"See you. Hi, Vijay. Bye, Vijay."

Vijay watched Dave go, a startled look in his eyes. "What was that all about?" he asked Derek.

"I'll tell you later," said Derek. "Come on. We've got studying to do."

The next morning was their science final. After managing to dent Gary's armor, Derek was in a better frame of mind than the day before. He smiled as he got down to work. Just the thought of making Gary eat humble pie was enough motivation to do his best—or even better! And he found the test easier than he'd thought it would be. He even finished with five minutes to spare!

Derek sat by himself, eating his lunch in the cafeteria. He usually sat with Vijay and some of his other friends, but today, he wanted to think about nothing but the task at hand.

He thought he'd done pretty well on the math and science tests. But this was a two-final day, which meant that after lunch, he had to take the English final. Not his best subject.

He sure hoped he'd beaten Gary on the first two tests.

Suddenly, Derek found that he'd lost his appetite. He packed his lunch back up and put it in his book bag.

It was time. The moment of truth had arrived.

• • •

Derek finished the grammar and vocabulary sections with no problem and was feeling better about things. He was about to tackle the essay that would count for 40 percent of his score when he looked up and saw that Gary was already handing in his finished test!

Derek glanced at the clock—only fifteen minutes left, and he hadn't even started his essay!

Suddenly all the confidence he'd been feeling drained out of him, as if the bottoms of his feet were full of holes. He felt the cold sweat coming on again.

Gary turned at the door and looked right at Derek, a huge grin sprouting on his face.

Was it that obvious that Derek was in trouble? Obviously yes. At least to Gary.

Time was running out on Derek. What was he going to write about? Ms. Terrapin had listed a few topics, but none of them had much appeal to Derek.

There was no time to think. He just had to make up his mind and start writing—*now!*

Okay, he told himself. *I'm just going to give it my best shot and try to relax, like my mom and dad always say to do.*

An Important Lesson I Have Learned

One important lesson I have learned in
my life is to enjoy every moment you can.
Sometimes I try so hard to succeed that I

get tense and worried. The weird thing about that is, then I usually don't do my best. I do my best when I am relaxed and having a good time. Even in the middle of some close ball games, I still enjoy myself.

When I mess up, I don't have to get even more tense because of it. I can remind myself that everyone messes up. I can learn from what I did wrong, so that I can do better next time.

Like with my friend Avery Mullins. She just started to play baseball this year, and she's really good. But being the only girl in the league gets her stressed out sometimes. And when she gets like that, she doesn't play her best ball.

That's a shame, because she's normally a really good player. I guess it's hard for her to relax when there are always kids making fun of her, just because she's the only girl on the team.

I can see she'd do better if she was playing loose. But it's harder to see it in myself. Sometimes I catch myself clenching my jaw, or making fists with my hands, and I have to tell myself to chill out.

Then there's my tied-for-best-friend Dave

Hennum. When he first moved to town, he was all tense because he didn't know anybody. So everybody thought he was a snob, and nobody liked him, and it just got worse and worse.

Once I got to know him, I realized he wasn't a snob at all. When he was relaxed and having fun, he was one of the coolest kids I've ever met, and we became best friends. We've got so much in common, like our dreams of being sports stars.

Well, we've been best friends ever since. But now he's moving away, and I'm really pretty tense about it. I don't know if we will even be friends in the future. I want to, but I have my doubts if it will work.

I am going to enjoy my last times with Dave, because you never know if you will have another chance to hang out with somebody you really care about. We are going to write to each other, so we'll see. Let's hope for the best.

But I don't know how not to be tense about saying good-bye.

Derek didn't know if his essay was any good, or if Ms. Terrapin would penalize him for not following one of the suggested topics—but what was done was done. He finished, putting down his pencil just as the bell rang.

At any rate, he'd enjoyed writing it. And at least every word in it was true.

Chapter Twelve

CRASH AND BURN

"Go get 'em, Sharlee!"

Derek yelled as loudly as he could, to make sure she heard him over the noise of the crowd. It was amazing how much noise parents could make when their kids were in action.

Sharlee spotted Derek and her mom in the stands and pointed at them, nodding confidently as she stepped up to the plate.

Just like a pro, Derek thought proudly.

Sharlee's team was up 3–2, with two runners on base. Hitting the first pitch, she drove them both in. It was a clean double—but Sharlee just kept on going, all the way around the bases, until she was finally tagged out at home!

She got mad, but only for a second. Then she leapt up and down along with her teammates, whooping it up to the max.

They're used to winning, Derek thought, watching Sharlee and her teammates celebrate. *They haven't lost once all year. Just like the Giants—before we ambushed them.*

Derek never liked to celebrate too much until the game was over, and the last out made. Because you never knew. In fact, Derek considered it bad luck. Like the great Yogi Berra once said, "It ain't over till it's over."

Sure enough, things started to fall apart for Sharlee's team in the fifth inning. Four straight batters hit the ball really hard. Sharlee made one spectacular catch on a line drive over her head—but she couldn't stop the onslaught alone, and her teammates made a couple of key errors in the infield to make the damage worse.

Looking at Sharlee, Derek could see that she was upset with what was happening—and particularly about the error. *She knows she would have made that play,* he thought.

By the time the inning was over, Sharlee's team was behind, 8–5. Derek couldn't see his sister's face, but he knew for sure that she was steaming mad. When her team went down one, two, three in the top of the sixth, Sharlee's magic carpet ride was over—she and her undefeated team had come crashing down to Earth.

Sharlee threw her mitt against the chain-link fence,

refusing to go shake hands with the winning team—until her dad knelt down beside her and said something in her ear, his hand on her shoulder. She angrily yanked herself free—but she did go over and shake hands, murmuring "Good game" like all the rest of her tearful teammates.

"Hey, slugger," Derek said when he caught up to her. "Don't get too down. You played a great game."

"No I didn't!" she shouted, still upset. "We lost!"

"Hey, it happens." Derek knew it wasn't what she wanted to hear. But it was the truth. "You did your best, and you did great—knocked in two runs, made a great catch—you almost had a homer there. That's pretty good for one game."

"Not for *me*! If we lose, that means we were *bad*! And *Daddy* messed *everything* up."

"What?"

"He put me at first base and moved everybody around and let Tara play shortstop."

"Sharlee, coaches *have* to play every player in every game. That's the rules. And hey, what about that catch you made?"

"So? We *lost*!"

"Come on, Sharlee. *Teams* lose or win games—not any one player or coach. And you won every other game you played! You know, *my* team's lost *three* games this year. You should be proud of yourself. And hey—didn't you have fun?" As he said the words, Derek could hear his dad's voice, telling him the same thing.

"I did have fun. Until today," Sharlee said, pouting, but calming down a little.

"I know, losing stinks—but that's baseball. You lose sometimes, no matter how good you are."

"I guess . . ."

"Listen, I think Dad's feeling bad. Maybe you should go say something to cheer him up. Maybe give him a hug, and a 'thank you' for doing such a good job."

"No! He was supposed to win us the championship, like he did for you!"

"He *tried*, Sharlee. He really did. Just like *you* did. And I'm sure he feels just as badly."

"Mmmm . . . okay." She turned to go.

"Hey, Sharlee?"

"Yeah?"

"Don't worry. The way you play? You're going to win a ton of championships."

That made her smile. "Thanks," she said, then ran to their dad. Derek watched as he got down on his knees to hug her, Sharlee's face buried deep in his shoulder.

A few minutes later, as the family was walking back to the car, Sharlee turned to Derek. "I'll comfort you when you lose too," she said, taking his hand.

"Aw, thanks, Sharlee. But who says we're going to lose, huh? I mean, what if we *win*?"

Sharlee shrugged. "Then at least Mommy and I won't have to change the cake—" She yanked her hand away, suddenly angry again. "*Aaaahhh!* Derek!"

"What?" he asked, his arms out. "What did I do?"

"You made me tell!"

"Tell *what*?"

"The *secret*! *Grrrr!*"

"I didn't make you do anything!"

"Yes, you did!"

So *that* was it—she and their mom were making him a special birthday cake! Derek resisted the urge to smile. He knew it would only make her madder. But now that she'd blown it, what could he do?

Luckily, the answer came to him. "You know what? I didn't even *hear* what you said, Sharlee."

"Yes, you did!"

"No, really! Because you were mumbling. What was it? Something about a *rake*? Or a *snake* or something?"

Sharlee looked at him, suspicious. "You *sure* you didn't hear?"

"Seriously."

"You swear?"

"Come on, Sharlee—tell me what you said. I can keep a secret."

"*No!* The secret is about *you*, silly!"

"Oh. . . . Come on, tell me—please. . . . *Pretty please.*"

"Never mind," she said, folding her arms in satisfaction. "You'll see when it's time."

That seemed to do the trick. He'd have to work on his surprised face in the mirror, just to make sure he did a good job when Sharlee gave him the cake.

He didn't normally like to deceive Sharlee, but in this case he decided to give himself a pass.

She seemed to be okay again at dinner. She and their dad went over all the great moments from their season, and by the time they'd finished dessert, Sharlee was in a fine mood.

She said, "Derek, you go into the living room—and promise to stay in there and NOT come into the kitchen. Mommy and I have work to do."

Derek's birthday was coming up that Sunday, and he guessed the *cake/rake/snake* was in process. He pretended not to be interested, focusing instead on reviewing for the standardized tests the next day.

It was almost eight o'clock when the phone rang. Mrs. Jeter picked it up. "Hello? Oh! Hello, Ms. Mullins."

Derek looked up. Avery's mother had called only once or twice before. Why was she calling *now*?

"Sure. . . . Oh, I see. . . . Is she all right?" Derek's mom was quiet for a long time, listening. Derek found himself making fists with his hands, and shook them out, blowing out a tense breath. *What could they be talking about?*

"Of course," said Mrs. Jeter. "He's right here." She held out the receiver. "Derek? Avery's mom."

Derek took the phone. "Hello."

"Derek, it's Samantha Mullins, Avery's mom."

"Uh-huh?"

"I had to take Avery to the doctor today."

"Oh . . ." Suddenly Derek felt something flip inside his stomach. "Is she . . . okay?"

"She'll be fine—but she has severe gastritis. Meaning a severely upset stomach. The doctor says it's stress-related."

"Uh-huh . . ." Derek tried to swallow, but his throat was too dry. He dreaded what was coming next.

"When Avery asked him about playing in the final on Saturday, he advised strongly against it. He feels it's the main source of her stress, that it's affecting her physical health, and that she needs a break from baseball. I'm sorry, but she won't be able to play Saturday. I've already told the coach, but Avery wanted me to let you know as well."

"Could I . . . could I talk to her?"

"I'm afraid she's too upset right now. But thank you for being her friend. I know how highly she thinks of you, Derek. And I'm so sorry. Please tell the team good luck from both of us."

"But—"

"I have to go. Avery needs me. Good-bye."

The phone went dead in his hands, and he put the receiver back on its cradle. "She's not playing Saturday," he told his parents, who were giving him curious looks.

"She's sick. Upset stomach. Her mom said it was caused by stress."

"Poor girl!" said Mrs. Jeter.

"Mom, will she be all right?" Derek asked.

"I'm sure she will, old man. She just needs some time to rest and recover."

Derek was relieved to hear that, at least. But what about the *team*? Avery had been one of their best players for the last half of the season!

How were the Yankees supposed to win without her?

Chapter Thirteen

BOILING POINT

Derek got more bad news on Thursday morning when the math and science finals results were handed out. Well, not *bad*, really. Studying with Vijay had sure helped. Derek had managed a 92 in math and an 88 in science.

But just as he'd suspected, those scores weren't good enough to beat Gary's.

"97 and 93," Gary mouthed silently from his desk. When Derek pretended not to understand, Gary held up his papers with the red circled numbers.

Derek had no choice but to hold his up in return. Gary raised both arms skyward in triumph and did a little dance in his seat.

But the news wasn't *all* bad, it turned out. Derek

did have one ace up his sleeve—he held up his English final. 95!

Gary's smile vanished. He froze mid-dance. When Derek shot him a questioning look, Gary held up his own paper: 92.

Now it was Derek's turn to do a desk dance. When the bell rang, the two boys went straight toward each other to compare notes.

"Two tests to one—I win!" Gary said, regaining his usual self-confidence.

"It's not over," Derek reminded him. "There's still the standardized tests. I can still come out on top."

"That's a laugh," Gary said with a snort. "Those tests measure *aptitude,* Jeter—as in, it doesn't matter how hard you study."

"I know what 'aptitude' means," Derek shot back.

"Then you should also know that no matter how hard you study—and I know you've been working your tail off to beat me—you still can't change your aptitude. IQ is IQ."

"Why don't we save the trash-talking till the final results are in?" Derek suggested.

"And by the way, how did you manage to get a 95 on the English test?" Gary snatched the paper from Derek's hands.

"Hey!"

Gary held it at a safe distance while he looked it over. "A hundred percent on the essay portion? Are you kidding me?"

Derek flushed with pride. He'd written that essay straight from his heart—and it had paid off big-time, staving off humiliation, at least for the moment.

"Here. Take your piece of trash back, speaking of trash-talk. I'll see you tomorrow." He handed back Derek's English final. "Boy, I can't wait to see you in that chicken suit. I hope you're excited. Better practice your chicken walk. Buck-buck—b'guck! You're goin' down, sucker!"

"We'll see about that," Derek said, trying to sound more confident than he felt. "We'll just see."

"I don't get these reading comprehension problems!" Derek shoved the booklet Vijay's way. "What would you say is the main point of the story? (A) acting on impulse is a mistake? Or (D) preparation is the key to success? I mean, they're *both* the point, aren't they?"

"Let me see that," Dave said, reaching out and taking the booklet. The three boys were grouped around the Jeters' kitchen table. Derek's parents and Sharlee were in the living room, giving them privacy to do their last-minute studying together.

It had been Vijay's idea to invite Dave to study with them. Derek had jumped at the chance to see his friend one extra time, and Dave had convinced his parents to let him put off packing one more afternoon.

"What about C?" Dave wondered. "That's a good answer too: it's important to expect the unexpected."

"Sheesh," Derek said, shaking his head. "You're right! They're all the right answer. Vij?"

"Well," said Vijay. "This is one I would definitely skip, and come back to when I'm done with all the other questions, yes?"

"Definitely," Derek agreed.

"For sure," said Dave.

Derek looked at his friend. What a bummer it was that the two of them had to spend most of their last moments together studying, instead of having fun!

You've got to enjoy every moment.

The words popped into his head. Was it his dad who'd said that? His mom? He wasn't sure—but Derek knew it was true. He also knew he wasn't doing a very good job of it just then. Enjoying every moment was way harder than it sounded! And the harder Derek tried, the harder it got!

Mrs. Jeter came in at eight forty-five to tell them Chase was there with the car and would be happy to drop Vijay off. The boys packed up their stuff and wished Derek good luck on the tests.

"Back at ya, guys," he said as they waved good-bye and left.

"You ready to call it a night, old man?" his mom asked him.

"Nah. Not yet. I've got to nail these tests. I'm just going to go as long as I can."

"Okay. Just don't stay up *too* late. You need your sleep, so you're rested and ready tomorrow."

When Derek next looked up from his books, it was almost his bedtime! But now he was hungry. He'd been too anxious to eat much dinner. His stomach was actually *hurting* now.

The image of Avery grabbing her stomach came into his head. Was *that* why she was hurting? Was she too stressed out to eat enough?

Derek made himself a PB and J sandwich and poured himself a glass of milk. He had just sat down to eat when his dad came into the kitchen. "Hey, champ," he said. "Studying make you hungry?"

"Mm-hmmph," Derek said, nodding with his mouth full.

His dad smiled and sat down across from him. "Well, finish up. It's bedtime."

Derek swallowed and took a swig of milk. "Ahh," he said. "I was so hungry, my stomach was actually *hurting*!"

"Hmm," said his dad, stroking his chin. "You think maybe all the pressure is starting to get to you?"

"Why do you say that?"

"Well, a lot of times when we're anxious about things, we feel it in our bodies. I notice you've been kind of tense lately . . . a little more irritable than usual . . ."

"Me?"

"Just a *little* more than normal," his dad reassured him.

"But it's understandable. Even Sharlee felt upset yesterday. That was a hard blow for her."

"She didn't mean it—about it all being your fault," Derek told his dad.

"Oh, I know that—but thank you for saying it. That's kind of you. And you seemed to know just what to say to settle Sharlee down too."

"Kind of." He guessed younger kids got over things more easily. They didn't have as many worries as big kids like him.

"Maybe you should say some of those same things to yourself, Derek. It helps to be able to shake off our worries, and just—"

"Enjoy the moment?"

"Exactly. You took the words right out of my mouth. You see what happened with your friend Avery? It's not good to get too wound up about things. I know you've got your big game Saturday. But you've been in big games before. And you'll be in bigger games down the road."

"It's not just that," Derek confessed. "There's the standardized tests, too."

"You've prepped as much as anyone could, Son. I'm sure you'll do fine."

"No, you don't understand, Dad—there's more." He proceeded to tell his dad all about his bet with Gary.

"Chicken suit, huh? Whew. That's rough."

"I'll say. Now I'm as good as doomed."

"Don't be so sure," said his dad. "All that work you've put in—I sense an upset coming."

Derek tried to smile. "Thanks, Dad. But it's hard to enjoy the moment right now."

"Derek, let me ask you—why do you put in so much effort in school? Not just now. I mean all the time."

"Huh? Well, uh, to get good grades!"

"And why do you need good grades?"

"To, uh, succeed in life as a grown-up?"

"That's right! And why do you put in the effort on the ball field? Taking swings and grounders all day, always the first one to show up, and the last one to leave?"

"Because one day I want to play shortstop for the Yankees—the real ones."

"And why do you want *that*?"

Derek thought for a moment. "Because . . . because I love playing baseball."

"*Bingo!* Never forget that, Derek! It's the most important part—because the road is always much longer than the time you spend at your destination. You've got to enjoy every moment you can along the way. That will give you the strength to keep on going, and to overcome the huge obstacles and struggles along the way."

"Avery's mom says that Avery's not going to play on Saturday," Derek said. "I guess it all got to her."

Mr. Jeter nodded sadly. "You see what can happen if you forget to relax and have fun? It's not healthy to be serious and intense every minute. Having fun and doing well go together—like breathing out and breathing in. One's no good without the other."

Derek shook his head. "Poor Avery. She wanted it so badly . . ."

His dad nodded. "A person can hold up only so much weight before they collapse," he said. "I guess she just took on too much."

Derek wondered if Avery would even show up to watch the team play on Saturday. He could imagine how agonizing it would be for her to just sit there and watch— especially if the Yankees wound up losing.

But how could she *not* come down to cheer the team on? Derek couldn't even imagine Avery not being there— not after everything they'd been through together!

Chapter Fourteen

BACK IN THE GAME

For a moment Derek wasn't sure where he was. It looked like Saint Augustine's school, but why wasn't anyone else there? Was it a weekend?

He heard a sound, like chalk on a blackboard. He tiptoed slowly down the hallway toward the source of the noise. And then he heard another sound, on top of the scratching. Was it . . . the clucking of a chicken?

He came to an open classroom door and looked inside. There, at the blackboard, was a giant chicken, scribbling "GARY PARNELL IS SMARTER THAN ME." Suddenly the chicken turned its head to look at Derek—and he saw that it had HIS FACE!

• • •

"AAAAAAAHH!"

Derek sat up in bed, his heart pounding. "A dream, that's all it was . . . just a *bad dream*."

Glancing at the clock, he saw that it was almost seven a.m. His alarm would be going off in six minutes.

Just as well. No way was he going to go back to sleep and risk having that dream again! If he got up and dressed now, he'd have time for a little last-minute review before heading off to school for the standardized tests.

After today it would all be over—except for the worst part. Tuesday was the last day of school—*doomsday*, in other words. Unless he could somehow beat Gary on *both* these exams, the chicken writing at that blackboard would be *him*!

Derek knew he had stiff competition in Gary. He could have kicked himself for taking the bait and one-upping Gary by suggesting the whole chicken suit thing!

Why had he done that? Writing on all the blackboards that Gary was smarter than him wouldn't have been too bad.

It would have been easy enough to just admit Gary's slightly superior IQ in the first place, and not have to deal with all his taunts. But Derek was not someone who could resist a challenge, no matter what the odds. And for that, he feared, he was about to pay the price.

Buck-buck-b'guck.

Math was in the morning, with English in the afternoon. Derek used the tricks Vijay had taught him to make sure he got through most of the questions quickly, with plenty of time at the end to go back and solve the difficult problems. He wound up with ten minutes to spare!

As he got up to leave for the cafeteria, Derek saw that Gary was still working away. *Well, well—that's a switch,* he thought happily. But then, as he left the room, he had second thoughts. Should he maybe have used those ten minutes to go over the tough questions one more time?

Dave was already in the cafeteria when Derek got there, and Derek sat down next to him.

"How'd it go for you?" Derek asked.

Dave shrugged. "I think I did pretty well—thanks to studying with Vijay."

"Yeah, right? That's probably why Gary always wants to make bets with me, not Vijay!"

They both laughed. It was true. Gary was the type of kid who would never make a bet he thought he could lose.

"So, listen," Dave said. "My mom told me we're moving Wednesday."

"So fast?" Derek said, dismayed. "That's the day after school's over!"

"I know," Dave said sadly. "I told you. They wanted to leave last week, but they put it off on account of me. So anyway, we're going to be packing and stuff next week. But I wanted to see if we could hang out one more time before we leave. Maybe over the weekend?"

"I'll ask my parents, but I think it'll be okay," Derek said.

"We could go drive some golf balls or something, maybe?"

"Sure."

Derek liked golf, but he avoided playing it during Little League season, so as not to mess up his baseball swing. But after Saturday? Why not?

"Wow, I just remembered," Derek said. "We're up against each other tomorrow!"

"I know. Should be fun, huh?" Dave smiled, but it faded quickly. "I . . . I know how much it means to you, Derek. I . . . I almost hope you guys win."

"Aw, you don't have to say that."

"I said '*almost*.' You know I play to win."

Derek knew, all right. "Hey, are you even going to be able to play golf in Hong Kong?"

"Oh yeah," Dave assured him. "The school even has its own golf team."

"Wow! Well, you're a cinch to make it, huh?"

"There are only ten kids in my class, so I have a feeling there's room on the team."

"It sounds fancy, but good. You must be excited."

Dave looked him right in the eyes. "I've never been as happy as I was here, in Kalamazoo," he said sadly. "It was hard at first—but I made real friends here—you most of all."

"Vijay and I are going to write you. Once a week. We're going to take turns."

"Oh. Okay, cool." Dave seemed doubtful, but Derek

knew now that he could write well when he wanted to—his essay had proved that.

Which gave him an idea. He reached into his book bag and pulled out his English final. Finding the essay page, he folded it in half and gave it to Dave.

"Here."

"What's this?"

"My English essay. Read it. Not now but later, when you're in Hong Kong."

The bell rang, and kids started filing into the cafeteria for lunch. Derek spotted Gary walking in, scanning the room for him.

"Ah, Jeter!" he said as he came over to gloat. "Gave up early this morning?"

"No, I finished the whole thing," Derek replied. "You seemed to be having some difficulty there."

"Ha! That's funny, Jeter. About as funny as you're going to look wearing a—"

He cut his words short, realizing that Dave was there. "Well, let me not ruin the surprise," he said, before tootling off toward the food line.

"What was that about?" Dave asked.

"I'll tell you next time I see you."

"Hmmm. Sounds intriguing." Dave waggled his eyebrows and stroked his chin.

Derek had to smile. It felt good, after all that studying and stress and worry, to have done his absolute best this morning. He had a pretty good feeling about this afternoon, too. After all, hadn't he already beaten Gary on the English final?

"Dad?"

"Yes, Derek?" Mr. Jeter looked up from the textbook he was reading.

"Could I ask you a favor?"

Mr. Jeter smiled. "I think you've chosen your timing for this ask wisely. You've been studying day in and day out for weeks, it seems like."

"Could you take me to the ball field early tomorrow, and hit me some grounders?"

Mr. Jeter nodded. "I'd like that, Derek. I'd have liked to be there more for you this season, but, well . . ."

"I know. *Sharlee.*"

"I think she has finally accepted that we didn't win the championship. It took her a while, but . . ." He paused, looking hard at Derek. "*You* ready to earn that big win tomorrow?"

"Of course!"

"That's my boy. We enjoy every minute, but we also play to win, right?"

"Right!"

By the time Coach Stafford arrived at the field with Pete, Derek and his dad had already been at it for thirty minutes.

Derek had worked up a sweat chasing ball after ball, but he had gotten a sort of rhythm going, as if he were on autopilot. Derek felt like if a ball came to him during the game, he could handle it with his eyes closed.

"I like it, I like it!" Coach K said. "That's some dedication there! Way to go, Derek!"

"Thanks, Coach. Thanks, Dad."

The coach then went over to the stands on the Tigers' side of the field. Sitting there was a man who'd shown up around fifteen minutes earlier. Next to him sat a kid in a Tigers uniform. Derek didn't know either of them, but Pete was talking to the kid like he knew him. *Probably from school*, thought Derek.

The man pointed over at Derek, and Coach K nodded. Derek wondered what they were saying about him.

"Hey, champ!" Derek's dad called. "Waiting on you!"

"Sorry, Dad." Derek got back into position to field another grounder.

Soon other kids from both teams started to filter in. Having dropped Derek and his dad off forty minutes ago, Derek's mom returned in the station wagon with Sharlee and Vijay, whose parents had to work this Saturday at the hospital.

The big black sedan showed up with Dave and Chase. Dave had been a really good player for their team the previous year. Chase had been Mr. Jeter's assistant coach—and those Tigers had won it all.

Derek looked around for Avery and her mom but didn't see them. *Maybe it's just too much for her,* he thought. Still, he knew that if it were *him*, he'd have shown up—for his team's sake, if nothing else.

Both teams got their warm-ups in and took batting practice. Once or twice Derek looked over at the man in the Tigers' stands and saw him taking notes. He wondered what that was all about.

The teams went to their benches. "Okay, everyone, let's gather around," Coach K said, waving his arms to beckon them. "First of all, I just wanted to say that we're going to be without Mullins today."

A moan went up from some of the players. "Her mom called to say she's sick. We all know how much she would want to be here."

That's when Derek saw Avery running toward them, mitt in hand, with her mom jogging behind her, trying to keep up.

"She's here!" Derek said. "Look!"

As the Yankees spotted her, they broke into cheers. Avery reached the circle and joined in the group hug. "Let's go!" she yelled.

The Yankees did their team cheer and broke the circle. Before Coach started reading out the lineup and positions, Derek found Avery and tugged on her shirt.

"Hey! I thought you weren't playing."

"Yeah, well . . ."

"Your mom said the doctor didn't want you playing anymore."

"I know what she said," Avery told him, a steely look in her eye. "I know what they *all* said. I told them I was playing today, no matter what happens after."

Derek was taken aback. "You sure you're going to be *okay*?"

"Don't worry about it," she snapped. "Not your problem, right?"

"I'm really glad you're playing, but I don't want to see you make yourself even sicker."

She nodded but didn't say anything. Derek knew why—for Avery this game was all about her brother. She would start thinking about herself again when the game was over.

"Well, all right!" Derek said. "Let's go out there and have a blast, huh?"

"Go, Yanks!" she replied.

"GO, YANKS!" they both yelled together.

Chapter Fifteen

REACHING FOR GLORY

The coaches and umpires met on the mound and shook hands. *This is it*, thought Derek. *The big game.*

He'd played mostly great all season, but if he messed up in *this* game, everything he'd done till now would go right up in smoke!

Derek shook off the negative thoughts. Time to quiet that little voice inside his head. Time to focus so sharply on the moment that there would be no room for the little voice—no room for doubt and fear.

He watched the Tigers take the field. Spotting Dave was easy, because of how tall he was. He wore number 17 and was playing third base.

Derek caught Dave's attention and tipped his cap in

a gesture of respect. Dave returned the gesture, smiling briefly before settling into fielding position.

"Come on, Mase!" Derek yelled as the Yankees' leadoff hitter stepped into the box.

"Play ball!" shouted the ump.

The Tigers' starter was the kid he'd seen in the stands before the game—with the man scribbling all the notes.

The pitcher went into his windup—and Derek saw the fastest pitch he'd seen all season. It sailed right by Mason, who swung *way* too late. Two pitches later Mason walked back to the bench, an easy strikeout victim.

Derek swallowed hard. He'd heard about this kid from Dave earlier in the season. If there was one reason the Tigers were now 7–2, Derek was now looking at him.

Derek let the first pitch go by, just to get a feel. It missed, low. But Derek knew he'd have to start his swing early if he wanted to catch up to the next one.

He fouled it off, and winced, mad at himself. Almost! On the next pitch he was ready even earlier—but the pitcher was smart as well as talented. He threw Derek a slow changeup. It made Derek look silly, finishing his swing before the ball hit the catcher's mitt. Again, Derek adjusted his thinking—but now he had no idea what would be coming.

It was a fastball, and Derek swung wildly, hitting nothing but air.

Two outs.

Pete, at least, managed to hit a fair ball—even if it was

only a grounder to second. And that was their first inning, going down one, two, three.

"Yeah!" Dave shouted, pounding his mitt. "Great job, Brad!"

The pitcher raised a hand in acknowledgment as he strutted back to the bench. Derek knew Brad was going to be a tough challenge for them all. But he promised himself he'd do better the next time he came up.

After grabbing his glove, he ran out to short and threw a couple of practice grounders to Avery at second, just to get loose. Harry threw his warm-up pitches, and the hitter came up to the plate.

Derek knew Harry liked to keep hitters guessing. Harry had a pretty good fastball. Nothing like Brad's, but above average. But his real skill was deception. He had a tricky changeup, along with a hesitation in his windup that threw batters' timing off.

When the leadoff man went down swinging on a full count, Derek let out a whoop. "Way to go, Harry!" he shouted.

Maybe Harry could match Brad, zeros for zeros. Maybe—if he was really at the top of his game . . .

But the next batter walked, and up came Brad. He worked the count even to 2–2, then laced a single to left center, sending the runner to third.

Next was Dave, looking focused and dangerous. Derek was impressed, proud that his friend had been named the

Tigers' cleanup hitter. Derek had worked with him on his game a lot, and Dave had sure come a long way in two years! When he'd first arrived in Kalamazoo, he'd had barely any baseball experience.

Dave lined one into the second-base hole. It looked like a sure hit—but Avery dived for it, snagged it on the short hop, checked the runner back to third, and flicked it to Derek at second. In stride he threw on to first, just in time to complete the double play!

A huge cheer erupted from the Yankees players and fans. The players practically ran back to the bench, excited to go on offense, and thrilled that the Tigers hadn't scored on what looked like a sure hit!

The cheer was matched by the moans from the Tigers side of the field. Dave, deprived of an RBI, walked slowly back to the bench, with a sad smile on his face. He pointed to Avery as he went. "Nice play!"

She pointed back at him, acknowledging the compliment.

"You too, Derek!" Dave added, pointing at him.

Derek touched the front of his cap as he sat down on the bench.

"Let's go!" Coach Stafford urged his team. "Make him throw strikes. We've got to run up his pitch count so he hits his limit early!"

Derek could tell Coach K didn't think the Yankees could score off Brad.

We'll see about that, he thought.

One thing was sure—in order to hit Brad's pitches, they had to *believe* they could.

Derek, for one, believed he could hit a*nybody*— especially if he'd already seen them once.

But did the rest of the Yankees believe?

They did take more pitches in the second inning, making Brad throw a bunch, but it didn't result in any base runners. Avery pounded the head of her bat into the ground when JJ struck out to end the frame, stranding her in the on-deck circle.

She would have had an at bat this inning, Derek knew. But because she'd shown up late, the coach had had to pencil her in at the last minute, and stuck her in the seventh slot instead of her usual fifth in the order. No wonder she was so frustrated.

Harry fared better in his half of the second. He did give up a single with two outs, but he put up another zero. And that was ultimately what mattered now.

Avery led off the third. The pitcher stared in at her for a really long time. Then he threw one inside that made her jump out of the way.

Some of the Yankees booed. Derek didn't think Brad was trying to hit her, just scare her—which was well within the rules—except he hadn't pulled that on any of the hitters who *weren't* girls.

Avery got right back in there, determined to show him

she wasn't afraid. When she lined the next fastball right back at him, it was Brad's turn to duck out of the way! The ball sizzled straight into center field for the Yankees' first hit of the game!

"WOO-HOO!" Avery yelled as she rounded first, clapping her hands. "Let's go!"

Unfortunately for the Yankees, giving up a hit to a *girl* seemed to make Brad angry—and his pitches even nastier. Vijay ducked out of the way on a called third strike. Tre' popped up to the catcher on a wicked changeup.

With two outs Mason hit a soft grounder down the line. But by the time the first baseman fielded it, Mason was already past him!

"SAFE!" called the ump.

Derek came up, with two out and two on, determined to have a better at bat this time. Brad started him off with a changeup, but Derek didn't bite. He worked the count to 2–1, then fouled off six straight pitches. He took another ball, fouled off three more pitches, and finally hit a screamer to second.

The fielder got his mitt on the ball, but it scooted a few feet away, and everyone was safe! *Bases loaded!*

Pete came up, taking some ferocious practice swings. "Easy . . . easy," Derek said under his breath, hoping Pete could read his thoughts.

But Pete was determined to hit one out of the park. He swung through two fastballs, then popped a changeup weakly back to the mound, leaving three Yankee runners high and dry.

Derek felt it like a punch to the gut. He could only imagine how *Avery* felt, with her stomach already hurting.

She sure wasn't letting on. Derek saw her kick the dirt as she got her mitt and headed out to second, as silent as the grave.

He sure hoped she was okay—that she'd be all right after this. Maybe it would have been better for her health if she hadn't played, but for his sake and the team's, he was sure glad she was out there right now!

Harry ran into trouble in the bottom of the third. He walked the leadoff man, who stole second when a pitch got away from JJ. When the next hitter walked, Coach K came trotting out to the mound to calm Harry down.

It seemed to work. He struck out the next batter, and then up came Brad again, with Dave on deck.

With a sweet swing, Brad hit a long fly to center. Mason caught it, but both runners tagged up and advanced on the play.

Could have been worse, thought Derek. Second and third with two out, and once again Dave coming to the plate in a critical spot.

Dave swung at the first pitch and lined it over Derek's head.

Derek leapt—*and came down with it!*

Dave let out a yowl and put his head in his hands. Once

again he'd been foiled by his best friend! And the Yankees had avoided doom by the skin of their teeth.

Dave looked at him and shook his head. Derek could see the frustration on his face, but Dave cared enough to give Derek his props with a pointed finger.

That made twice this game, Derek thought with satisfaction—though he wished it hadn't been Dave he'd frustrated.

"Keep making the pitcher work!" Coach Stafford told his troops. "We've got to make this inning his last!"

Harry got them started, running up a full count before swatting a clean double down the left field line. Ryan followed by working a walk.

The pitches were starting to pile up for Brad, but he didn't seem any the worse for wear. His pitches were still whistling in, faster than a speeding bullet.

JJ couldn't stand up to those fastballs, and after battling for seven pitches, he went down swinging. Then up came Avery.

Derek saw Brad dig in extra deep, wanting more than anything else to show up this girl, who'd had the nerve to embarrass him by getting a hit off him!

He buzzed her again on the first pitch—but if he thought that would scare Avery, he had no idea who he was dealing with. She edged even closer to the plate and hit the next pitch so hard, it glanced off the first baseman's glove and bounced six feet away from him!

It became a footrace to first between Avery and Brad, who was hustling over to take the throw. They got there at the same time and collided! Avery went flying into foul territory, while Brad fell the other way, dropping the ball!

"Safe!" cried the ump. "Everybody's safe!"

Avery got up, dusted herself off, and yelled "YEAH!" looking straight at Brad, who certainly wasn't going to apologize. It might have been a rough play, but it was a clean one, and they both knew it.

Bases loaded now, with only one out. Vijay swung at the first pitch and hit a pop foul that the Tigers' catcher caught easily.

Now it was up to Tre'. He took two strikes, then stroked a looper down the left field line! Derek thought for sure it would drop in for a double—but Dave launched himself into the air, reached out to the full extent of his tall frame, and made the leaping catch!

Derek groaned in agony, along with all his teammates and the Yankees' fans.

This was too much! How many men had they left on base already? Derek knew scoring chances didn't grow on trees.

He took a moment to point to Dave. "Great play, man."

Dave smiled. "Now we're even." He blew out a deep breath, as if to say, *Some game, huh?*

Incredibly, the game was still scoreless. But it didn't stay that way for long.

Chapter Sixteen

FIGHT TO THE FINISH

Harry had stood tall on the mound for three straight innings, but he'd spent a lot of pitches doing it. He worked the first hitter to a 3–2 count—with the two strikes being long drives that fell just foul.

Not wanting to walk the leadoff man, Harry then grooved a so-so fastball, right down the plate. The hitter pounced on it, driving it to right center for a ringing double!

Derek saw his two coaches talking in low voices, looking over at Harry. They had to be deciding whether to pull him now or leave him in. In the end, they stayed with him.

It turned out to be the wrong move. Harry fell behind in the count again, then had to throw one over the middle.

The batter hit it on the nose for another double—scoring the first run of the game!

Harry kicked the dirt, disgusted with himself. It was just one run, but this late in the game, it felt like they were down ten runs, not one.

"Hang in there, Harry!" he shouted. "Let's go!" No way was Derek going to let his team go down in defeat—not without a fight!

Harry was tiring, that much was obvious. But the coaches kept him in there, hoping their best pitcher could stop the bleeding.

Sure enough, Harry rallied to strike out the next man for the first out of the inning.

Facing the Tigers' number eight hitter, Harry got ahead in the count, 0–2. "Come on, Harry!" Derek shouted. "No batter, no batter!"

Harry nodded, pulled the bill of his cap down over his eyes, reared back, and threw. The hitter sent a ground ball the opposite way. It wasn't hit hard, but it was placed perfectly between Avery and Ryan. It skittered between them into right field, and the Tigers' second run scored!

Coach K practically ran out to the mound—as if it weren't already too late. "Mullins!" he called, motioning for her to take the mound.

As the downcast Harry walked to the bench, Coach K handed Avery the ball. "You okay?"

She nodded vigorously, staring into space, in a world of her own.

"Okay, kid. It's showtime." He clapped her on the back and headed for the dugout, shaking his head.

Avery blew out a big breath, then toed the rubber, staring in at the catcher. She wound up, then fired a fastball over the inside corner.

The hitter backed away, but the ump yelled, "Strike one!"

Avery took the return throw and got right back onto the rubber. She was breathing hard, all intensity and fire. The next pitch was a changeup, and the hitter swung early, catching only air.

"Strike two!" the ump called.

The Yankees fans were cheering their hearts out, but the players behind Avery didn't make a sound. They were all holding their breaths.

Avery fired a fastball, high and outside. Protecting the plate with two strikes, the hitter reached for it, and hit a grounder straight to Derek. He flipped to second for one, and the throw to first was in plenty of time to complete the double play.

Inning over!

"YAAAAAHHHH!" Avery screamed, pumping her fist repeatedly as she marched back to the bench, still staring straight ahead.

Derek grinned and shook his head in admiration. He

liked to think of himself as an intense competitor. But Avery? She took the cake!

"Okay, team, let's get those runs back!" Coach K shouted, clapping his hands in encouragement.

Mason was up first—top of the order—and Derek was optimistic. They had the right guys up to start a rally.

Even better, the Tigers had a new man on the mound.

Thank goodness! Derek thought. He hadn't been relishing the thought of having to face Brad again, who was now playing first base, having reached his pitch limit.

Mason saw six pitches before popping up to short center. It was enough for Derek to determine that this pitcher wasn't nearly as intimidating as Brad.

Derek stepped confidently into the box. He knew this was probably his last at bat of the season, and he was determined to get a rally started.

Be smart, he told himself. *We're two runs down. You can't win it with one swing. Just get on base.*

He let one strike go by, just to get the timing right. Then, on a 2–1 count, he hit a chip shot over the first baseman's head. Derek didn't stop running until he was on second base!

"Let's GOOO!" he roared, clapping his hands together so hard that it hurt. "Come on, Pete! Keep the line going!"

Derek hoped Pete got the message. Pete was always trying to hit home runs—and as a result he struck out a lot. The Yankees couldn't afford that now.

One thing about Pete, though—he was big and intimidating. The pitcher must have been at least a little scared, because everything he threw him was away.

He wound up walking Pete, who jogged down to first muttering to himself, frustrated that he hadn't gotten anything to hit.

Next up was Elliott, batting for Harry. Elliott had never been much of a hitter, but Derek knew the rules. They said that everyone on the team had to play at least two innings in the field, and bat at least once. It was the same for the Tigers. The rules were the rules, and you went to war with the troops you had left.

Elliott joked around a lot during practices, and even during games. But he was dead serious now. He looked terrified—of the moment, if not the pitcher. He let two strikes go by, hesitating as he started to swing. Then he swung too early at a changeup—and whiffed.

Two outs. Cooling his jets at second, Derek felt the tension rising inside him again. They couldn't afford to let this rally go by—not with the heart of their order batting!

Ryan was next—one of their best hitters, for sure. Coming through in the clutch, he belted one to deep right that no fielder in the league could have caught! Derek raced around to score the Yankees' first run. Behind him came Pete, just in time to beat the relay, while Ryan coasted in to third with a stand-up triple!

Tie game—and the Yankees weren't through yet!

Derek knew he was screaming, but he couldn't even hear himself, surrounded as he was by the crush of his happy teammates outside the dugout.

Miles came up to bat for JJ—another substitution. Miles had power, even if he did strike out a lot. This time, though, he didn't need to even swing. The Tigers pitcher, clearly rattled by Ryan's game-tying blast, had lost the strike zone completely. He plunked the hitter right in the shoulder. Miles jogged down to first, wincing a little as he rubbed his shoulder, and the rally continued.

Derek turned to watch Avery as she entered the batter's box. It was all on her shoulders now. *Could she handle the weight?*

The pitcher had already seen what she could do with the bat. On the other hand, he didn't want to walk her and load the bases.

The count ran full. Then Avery fouled off three straight pitches, before getting the one she wanted, and ripping it into right—for a single that scored the go-ahead run!

The Yankees went crazy while the Tigers and their fans moaned in dismay. Avery was jumping up and down at first, excited beyond belief.

Vijay struck out to end the half inning, but nothing could dampen the Yankees' spirits now. They'd come from behind late in the game yet again—and now they were just six outs away from pay dirt! All they had to do was hold the Tigers.

But Dave's team wasn't 7–2 for nothing. Though down, they were not defeated. And they had the top of their order coming up in the fifth.

Avery got the first out easily enough, with Pete scooping up a two-hopper and throwing on to first in plenty of time.

Things certainly seemed to be going the Yankees' way. But baseball is a quirky game. Sometimes funny bounces happen. Derek was reminded of this fact when the next hitter cued a ball off the end of the bat. It took a crazy bounce, and wound up as an infield hit.

Okay, no problem, thought Derek. "Let's get two!" he shouted.

But it wasn't Avery at second base now—it was Norman.

The next batter hit a sharp grounder right at him, so sharply that Norman ducked, reaching in vain for the ball as it sizzled past him. As a result, the Tigers wound up with men on first and second, bringing the pressure on Avery and the Yankees to a boil.

Derek could see it in her face, and in her body language. He glanced over to the stands, and saw Avery's mom standing in the back row of the bleachers. She looked like she wanted to run onto the field and rescue her daughter.

He knew Avery might not appreciate it, but he decided to go over and say something to her. Just something to lighten the moment a little. "Hey! That kid Brad is up next. Give him that funky delivery of yours. It'll mess him right up."

"What funky delivery?" she asked, distracted from whatever she'd been thinking.

"You know," said Derek, doing a little imitation with his elbows out like a chicken. "Like you do sometimes on the Hill, for kicks?"

Incredibly, she let out a laugh. "Oh yeah—that one. Good idea."

Derek went back to short, satisfied that he'd done the right thing. At least he'd given her something else to think about. Something she could *do*—a surprise she could spring that would put her in the driver's seat and keep Brad off-balance.

Avery threw out her elbows like a chicken, paused a second at the height of her motion, then threw an absolute dart that went right by the dazed Brad for a strike!

He shook his head disgustedly, then dug in, ready for more of the same. Instead Avery quick-pitched him, catching him flat-footed for strike two! She quick-pitched again on the next pitch, but this time it was a changeup, and Brad swung right through it! He went back to the bench in a rage, yelling at himself.

"One more out, Ave!" Derek called to her. "You got this!"

Dave was up next. *His last at bat ever in Kalamazoo,* Derek realized with a pang of sadness.

Avery used her funky motion again, and Dave managed only a weak bouncer to first. Ryan was waiting for it behind the bag—and it should have been an easy third out.

But once again, a quirky bounce went against the Yankees. The ball hit the bag and ricocheted into foul territory! By the time Ryan retrieved it, the tying run had scored, and the Tigers had runners on second and third!

Avery looked down at the ground, distraught. She turned in every direction, as if to ask, *Why?* But Derek knew there was no answer to that question.

Coach K came out and talked with her. Derek could hear him asking her if she was okay. Avery looked away from him, wincing but insisting she was fine. Coach K looked over to the stands, where Avery's mom was standing and anxiously wringing her hands.

That seemed to decide things for Coach K. He took the ball from Avery, leaving it up to Pete to get the Yankees out of this jam. Avery shuffled slowly back to the bench. All the anger, all the fight had drained out of her. She looked *beaten.*

Pete hadn't prepared for this moment. But he was the best hope they had to keep it tied, and snatch victory from the jaws of defeat.

No such luck. The first hitter Pete faced doubled to left, scoring two runs and putting the Tigers ahead 5–3. Derek's whole body sagged as he watched them mob each other, already celebrating.

Go ahead, celebrate, he thought. *You haven't won yet.*

The Tigers weren't done, though. They put two more runs across before Pete finally got the last out. The inning had been a total disaster, leaving the Yankees four runs down with only three outs left!

Norman, their number nine hitter, led off. He promptly popped back to the pitcher for the first out. Then Mason hit a grounder that he almost beat out for another hit—but a great throw from Dave across the infield just nipped him in time.

Derek was the team's last hope, and he waited patiently for his pitch. When it came, on a 3–1 count, he laced it to left for a clean single. "Come on, Pete!" he yelled, trying to muster the enthusiasm he'd felt an inning ago.

Pete did manage to hit one hard—but the pitcher stuck out his mitt, and the ball smacked right into the pocket and stayed there!

One last cruel twist of fate, and the game was over!

Derek stood on first base, stunned. He couldn't believe the season had come to such a sudden, disastrous end!

All the Yankees were somber, hugging each other sadly as they watched the Tigers go wild with joy. Their coach was already dragging a big box of trophies onto the field to give his champions.

The teams shook hands, but Avery remained on the bench alone, her head buried in her hands.

"Great game," Derek told Dave as they shook.

"It really was, wasn't it?" Dave said. "Sorry one of us had to lose."

"Me too. Hey, you played great, though. Seriously."

"You did too. You robbed me twice! I just wish . . ."

But there was no time to talk now. Other kids were pushing forward behind them. "See you Monday at school, I guess," Dave said.

"What about going to the range this weekend?" Derek asked.

"I know we talked about it," Dave said. "But I'm way behind with my packing, and my folks are getting pretty annoyed about it. So . . ."

"Okay," Derek said. "But if you do get free—"

"I'll call you," Dave said. "You know I will."

After the handshakes, Derek went over to Avery and sat next to her. Seeing him there, she reached over and hugged him. Derek could tell she was holding back all the fury and frustration she felt.

"You did everything you could," he told her. "Just some bad bounces, that's all. Your brother would have been proud of you. No—he *is* proud. You *know* he is. We'll get him that trophy next year. You'll see."

But even as he said it, he knew there might not be any next year for Avery. She'd been through a lot this season, taken a lot of abuse and neglect, and put a world of pressure on herself to honor her brother's legacy. After today would she come back and try again?

Should she even?

After a moment she got up and silently walked off toward the stands. Her mother was waiting there, along with Avery's brother's two friends.

Derek found his own family. They all had kind words for him, but they knew how disappointed he was, and didn't try to sugarcoat a bitter, bitter defeat. Hugging them all, Derek felt better than he had a minute before.

He knew why, too—everything he'd just told Avery went for him as well. He'd played his heart out and had a really good game. It just hadn't been *enough*.

But there would be another game for him, another season, and, thinking optimistically, another championship game. Besides, he'd learned a ton this year, even though they'd come up short in the end.

Most important, it really had been *fun*—most of the time, at least. He'd made a great new friend in Avery, and he'd become a better ballplayer along the way.

He made the rounds of his teammates, telling them to hold their heads up because they'd had a great season and should be proud of what they'd accomplished. And as he said it, he realized it was true.

"Derek!" he heard his dad calling.

Derek turned and saw that Mr. Jeter was standing with the man who'd been sitting in the bleachers taking notes. "Come on over here, old man," his dad said.

Derek walked over to them. "This is Mr. Russell," his dad said. "He'd like to talk with you for a minute."

"Hi," said Derek. "Nice to meet you."

The man stuck out his hand. "Great game, young man.

"Derek," Derek said, shaking it. "Derek Jeter."

"Rick Russell. My son Brad was the starting pitcher?"

"Oh yeah," Derek said, looking over at Brad, who was celebrating with Dave and the rest. "He's tough to hit."

"He's going to be on the traveling team this fall."

"Oh yeah? Cool."

"I know because I coach the team."

Derek's eyes widened. He'd heard of the traveling team's exploits. They'd had a winning record four years running!

But why was Mr. Russell telling him all this?

"I'd like you to think about trying out, if you're interested."

"Me?"

"Only the best players make it, but I think you have a fighting chance."

"Wow! Thanks, Mr. Russell!" Derek blurted out. "I mean . . ." He looked up at his dad, who was beaming with pride. "I mean, if my parents say it's okay."

"Your mom's over there, talking with Mrs. Mullins," Mr. Jeter said. "Why don't you go ask her? If she says yes, it's all right with me."

"Yessss!" Derek said excitedly. "Nice meeting you, sir," he told Mr. Russell.

"Nice meeting you, too, Derek," said the coach. "You play a great shortstop, you know? I really like your game. More importantly, I like your approach. I saw you taking grounders with your dad. You were here a half hour early. That's dedication." He shook Derek's hand again. "I look forward to the next time we meet. You can find notices about tryouts at your school. We post information on all the lobby bulletin boards." Shaking hands with Derek's dad, he added, "Mr. Jeter? It's been a pleasure." Then he turned and walked over to the Tigers' side of the field.

Derek stared after him, as if he'd just seen a shooting star flare across the sky. Finally he shook himself back to Earth. He turned to go find his mom and ask her permission to try out. She was still there in the stands—but Avery, her mom, and her entire cheering section had vanished.

Chapter Seventeen

END OF THE SEASON

Derek's mom and sister had already gone home, having been offered a lift with Chase, who said he'd drop them off on his and Dave's way home. Derek now sat in the back seat of the family station wagon with Vijay, who for once was silent and somber. He almost always looked on the bright side, but this defeat had been crushing, for all the Yankees. There was no getting around it.

Mr. Jeter didn't break the silence. He let the boys have their private time, to process what had just happened. He'd lost big games before, and he knew what it was like.

Derek, though, had something new and intriguing to distract him from his misery. The conversation with Coach Russell had taken him completely by surprise. Now it offered something hopeful to look forward to, instead of having to dwell on this painful loss.

After they dropped Vijay off, his dad pulled into the family parking spot in front of their townhouse. "You okay?" his dad asked.

"I guess I'll get over it."

"Come on inside. Let's get some lunch, huh?"

They went inside. As Derek stepped through the doorway, he heard, *"SURPRISE!"*

There were his mom, Sharlee—and his aunt Julie! Sharlee and his mom were holding a big tray with a cake on it!

"HAPPY BIRTHDAY!" everyone shouted.

"W-wait! My birthday's not till tomorrow!"

"Sharlee couldn't wait," Mrs. Jeter explained.

"Mommy, aren't we going to sing?" Sharlee said, tugging at her mother's shirt.

The whole family broke into song. As they serenaded him, Derek took a closer look at his cake. It was homemade, in the shape of a baseball diamond. On the infield was written in icing: HAPPY BIRTHDAY, DEREK! Underneath was the number twelve, for how old he was.

In the outfield there was an interlocking *NY* for the Yankees, and the word "CHAMPIONS" under it. Above, in a different-color icing, was written in small letters "almost."

"Wow!" he cried when the song was over. "I can't believe this cake!"

"Make a wish and blow out the candles!" Sharlee ordered.

He did as he was told, and then they all marched into the kitchen to watch Mrs. Jeter cut the cake.

"Aunt Julie! I didn't know you were coming!" Derek said, giving her a big hug.

"I wouldn't miss my nephew's birthday," she said, kissing him on the cheek.

"So, Sharlee," Derek said, "this is why you've been acting so suspicious the past two weeks!"

She giggled with pleasure. "Mommy and I made the cake all by ourselves!" she bragged. "And I helped paint the players, too! See? You're the one at shortstop!"

Derek looked closer. "It does kind of look like me. Only handsomer. Great job, Sharlee. You're an artist! And you sure know how to keep a secret."

Sharlee beamed with pleasure. "Can we give Derek his presents now?"

"Sharlee," her dad teased, "wouldn't you rather have your cake first?"

"No. *Now!*" Sharlee protested. "Daddy, pleeeeze?"

"All right, all right," Mr. Jeter said, laughing. "You've been very patient for two whole weeks, so . . ."

There were two envelopes, a medium box, and a small box. Derek opened the first envelope. It was a card, and inside were tickets to see the Detroit Tigers play the Yankees the following weekend at Tiger Stadium!

"WOW!" Derek said. "This is amazing! Thanks, Mom! Thanks, Dad!"

He gave them all hugs and kisses. It was the best present he could have asked for!

He opened the next card. It was from his grandparents in New Jersey. "We can't wait to see our great big grandson," his grandma had written. "And guess what? We're going to the Hall of Fame together in July!"

Derek couldn't believe it! He'd always wanted to see the Baseball Hall of Fame in Cooperstown, New York— and now he was going to go!

He couldn't wait to see what was in the medium-size box. . . . A brand-new mitt! "Thanks!" he said, trying it on. "I really need this. My old one's about to fall apart."

"That's what happens when you use a mitt as much as you do," his dad commented. "Wear it in good health."

"This one is from me," said Aunt Julie, handing Derek the small box.

He opened it to find a metal object wrapped in tissue paper. It was a gold chain, with a gold interlocking *NY* pendant hanging from it!

It took Derek's breath away.

"I . . . I don't know what to say." Derek draped the pendant around his neck and glanced at the mirror by the front door. "It's beautiful. Thanks, Aunt Julie. You're the best!"

"Aunt Julie had it specially made for you," Mrs. Jeter said.

"That's right," said Aunt Julie. "It's a reminder that your whole family is behind you." She kissed him on the cheek again. "We're all so proud of you, Derek. You're really growing up."

Sharlee nestled close to him on the couch. "Even though Mommy did the writing on the cake, it was me who put in the 'almost,' so you wouldn't feel so bad about losing."

"Aw, Sharlee . . . ," Derek said, putting his arm around her shoulder.

"That's why it's so messy. We had to get home before you, and I had to rush, so . . ."

"I'm sorry you had to change it," Derek told her. "It would have been perfect the other way."

"Don't feel bad, Derek," Sharlee told him. "Even the best teams lose sometimes. Even mine! Even when Daddy coaches! Right, Daddy?"

Mr. Jeter laughed, shaking his head. "Yup. Can't argue, Sharlee, you're quite the philosopher."

"Huh?" Sharlee said, confused. "What's a philofficer?"

That made the whole family crack up.

Leave it to Sharlee, thought Derek. *She could put* any-body *in a better mood!*

"Oh, and there's one more surprise," said Mrs. Jeter. She went to the front door and opened it. "You boys can come in now."

"SURPRISE!" Vijay and Dave shouted as they burst through the door. "Happy birthday, Derek!"

"I can't believe this!" Derek said. "It just keeps getting better!"

"I'll cut you all a slice of cake," said Aunt Julie. She picked up the cake and took it into the kitchen.

"Don't you want to know what our present to you is?" Vijay asked.

"Okay, I'm game," Derek said. "What is it?"

"As soon as we're done scarfing down your cake, Chase is driving us over to the golf range!" said Dave.

Derek laughed. "You said you were going to be too busy."

"Well," Dave said, "it was all part of the surprise, so . . ."

"You guys are too much," Derek said, smiling and shaking his head. "Okay, Dave. You asked for it. I'm going to outdrive you by at least ten yards. You wait and see!"

Standardized test results were handed out on Monday. As he watched Ms. Terrapin go around the class handing out the results, Derek could feel a lump of fear rising in his throat.

This was it. He could already feel the chicken suit weighing heavily on his shoulders as he wrote "Gary Parnell is smarter than me" on every blackboard in the school.

Gary sure seemed pleased with his grades. He looked over at Derek, who still hadn't gotten his. Gary smiled with evil anticipation.

Ms. Terrapin handed him his results. 695 and 670! Derek was surprised and pleased to see that he was in the 97th percentile in math and 95th in English. He only hoped it was good enough . . .

Class was dismissed at noon, as it would be the following day, the last day of the school year. Derek cleaned out his desk and headed for his locker, where Gary was waiting for him.

"Well? Let's see 'em, Jeter!"

"You first."

Gary shrugged. "Why not? Read 'em and weep, my friend."

Gary showed Derek his grade sheet.

Derek couldn't believe his eyes—686 and 665!

"Nice job, Gar," he said. "Now check these grades out! Buck-buck-b'guck!"

Gary's eyes grew as wide as saucers as he read the fateful numbers. *"WHAT? NO WAY!"*

"Amazing, huh?" Derek said, which was exactly how he felt—surprised and exhilarated, but mostly relieved.

"This is baloney!" Gary complained, shoving Derek's grades back at him.

"What happened to 'aptitude,' Gar? I guess we know for sure now which one of us is smarter, huh?"

"Give me a break," Gary scoffed.

"I don't think so. I don't think I'll do that."

"Seriously, Jeter? You *know* standardized tests are totally bogus!"

"You didn't think so till now. Anyway, we made a bet, and you lost."

"No way. I'm not doing this!" Gary turned to go.

"Waaaaiit a minute," Derek interrupted. "What about tomorrow? Writing on the blackboards? The *chicken suit*?"

"Nah, I don't think so."

"Oh, come on, now," Derek said, getting angry. "If *I* had lost, you wouldn't have let *me* off the hook."

"Maybe not," Gary admitted. "But I know for a fact that I'm smarter than you, Jeter. So there's no way I'm going to write a lie on the blackboards, let alone dress up in a chicken suit!"

"Where's your sense of honor? We had a deal!"

Gary shrugged and offered Derek a sickly smile. "Honor, shmonor," he said. "When it comes to chicken suits, I'm camera shy."

"You know I beat you fair and square!" Derek called after him as Gary sauntered away.

It really burned him that Gary had welched on their bet! He knew he would have honored his word no matter how painful it was. But Gary wasn't Derek—and thank goodness for that!

He sighed, feeling proud and contented. It didn't really matter so much in the end what Gary did. The whole school might not get to know who was smarter. But *Gary* knew. And most important, *Derek* knew.

From now on Gary would never be able to lord it over him again!

All the sweat and suffering had been worth it, Derek

thought. *Good old Vijay*. If it hadn't been for his help . . . and it wasn't just the test-taking tips. He'd kept Derek sane the whole time they'd been studying.

Sure, Dave was moving away. But Derek still had one best friend. He lived just down the footpath. And he'd still be here.

Derek was already standing at home plate on the Hill when the black sedan drew up to the curb and Dave hopped out with his mitt and bat.

"What's up?" he wondered, looking around. "Where is everybody?"

Derek shrugged. "I guess they've got other stuff going on."

They started throwing the ball back and forth, waiting for someone else to show up so they could have more of a real game. But no one came.

After half an hour Dave said, "I guess I should get on home."

"Oh. Okay. Will I see you again before you go? Maybe go drive some more balls?"

Dave looked down. "I don't think so," he said. "My room's still a disaster area."

"So . . . I guess I won't see you again for a long time," Derek said. The sudden realization hit him. *This was it.*

He hugged Dave hard. "I'll write to you. Next week."

"Me too," said Dave, trying not to choke up. "I promise."

"Me too. Shake?"

"Shake."

"And you know I'm always here for you," Derek added as they went through the steps of their handshake.

"Same here," said Dave.

They hugged again, one last time. "See ya, Dave."

"See ya." Derek watched Dave turn and head back to the car. It pulled away and shrank into the distance, leaving him standing there, alone.

But no—not quite alone. . . .

Looking up the Hill, Derek saw a familiar figure, wearing a baseball cap and waving to him.

Avery!

"Hey," he greeted her. "How are you?"

"Better," she said. "The doc gave me some medicine, and I've been taking it really easy, so . . ."

"Good. Good. . . . I was kind of worried there for a while."

She shrugged off his concerns. "I'm fine now. No big deal."

"I knew you'd show up for the game. Even when your mom and the doctor said you couldn't."

She smiled. "Thanks. I talked them into it."

Derek smiled too. He could imagine what that conversation must have been like!

"I saw Dave go," she said suddenly.

"Yeah." Derek sighed heavily.

"So . . . that's it, huh?"

"Guess so."

"Sorry. It stinks to lose a friend."

"We're going to stay in touch."

"Uh-huh. Great." She nodded, but not like she believed it. "So, what are you doing this summer?"

"Going to my grandparents' in New Jersey. We go every year, my sister and I. It's fun. Lots of cousins our age. The lake . . . and we're going to visit the Hall of Fame in Cooperstown, too."

"Cool," she said, sounding faintly disappointed. "See you in the fall, then, I guess."

"You going to play next year?" he asked.

"Yeah," she answered. "Basketball, soccer."

"Oh."

"And baseball, too, next spring, of course."

"Really?" Derek was surprised. "That's great! I mean, I'm glad. You going to try again to win it for your brother?"

She shook her head. "Nah. I tried that, and it was too much for me. Next year it's going to be for *me*."

"That's good. That's *really* good. I mean, it's all about having fun in the end, right?"

"You got that right," she replied, giving him a broad smile. "So . . . you got time for a catch?"

JETER PUBLISHING

Jeter Publishing's eighth middle-grade book is inspired by the childhood of Derek Jeter, who grew up playing baseball. The middle-grade series is based on the principles of Jeter's Turn 2 Foundation.

Jeter Publishing encompasses adult nonfiction, children's picture books, middle-grade fiction, ready-to-read children's books, and children's nonfiction.

JETER'S LEADERS

is a leadership development program created to empower, recognize, and enhance the skills of high school students who:

◇ **PROMOTE HEALTHY LIFESTYLES AND ARE FREE OF ALCOHOL AND SUBSTANCE ABUSE**

◇ **ACHIEVE ACADEMICALLY**

◇ **ARE COMMITTED TO IMPROVING THEIR COMMUNITY THROUGH SOCIAL CHANGE ACTIVITIES**

◇ **SERVE AS ROLE MODELS TO YOUNGER STUDENTS AND DELIVER POSITIVE MESSAGES TO THEIR PEERS**

"Your role models should teach you, inspire you, criticize you, and give you structure. My parents did all of these things with their contracts. They tackled every subject. There was nothing we didn't discuss. I didn't love every aspect of it, but I was mature enough to understand that almost everything they talked about made sense." —DEREK JETER

DO YOU HAVE WHAT IT TAKES TO BECOME A
JETER'S LEADER?

- ◇ I am drug and alcohol free.
- ◇ I volunteer in my community.
- ◇ I am good to the environment.
- ◇ I am a role model for kids.
- ◇ I do not use the word "can't."
- ◇ I am a role model for my peers and younger kids.
- ◇ I stand up for what's right.

- ◇ I am respectful to others.
- ◇ I encourage others to participate.
- ◇ I am open-minded.
- ◇ I set my goals high.
- ◇ I do well in school.
- ◇ I like to exercise and eat well to keep my body strong.
- ◇ I am educated on current events.

CREATE A CONTRACT

What are your goals?

Sit down with your parents or an adult mentor to create your own contract to help you take the first step toward achieving your dreams.

For more information on JETER'S LEADERS, visit
TURN2FOUNDATION.ORG

About the Authors

DEREK JETER played Major League
Baseball for the New York Yankees for twenty
seasons and is a five-time World Series cham-
pion. He is a true legend in professional sports
and a role model for young people on and off
the field and through his work in the community with his Turn 2 Foundation. For more
information, visit Turn2Foundation.org.

Derek was born in New Jersey and moved
to Kalamazoo, Michigan, when he was four.
There he often attended Detroit Tigers games
with his family, but the New York Yankees
were always his favorite team, and he never
stopped dreaming of playing for them.

PAUL MANTELL is the author of more
than one hundred books for young readers.

BULLYING.
BE A LEADER AND STOP IT.

TURN THE PAGE FOR A SNEAK PEEK AT

SWITCH-HITTER.

NEW YORK TIMES BESTSELLING AUTHOR

DEREK JETER

SWITCH-HITTER

"Hey, old man. It's Vijay on the phone—for you!"

Derek Jeter dropped the pile of folded clothes he'd been holding. They fell right back into the suitcase he'd been unpacking, and he hurried downstairs to pick up the phone from his mom.

"Hey, Vij!" he said breathlessly. "How's it going?"

"It's all good now that *you're* back," said Vijay with a little laugh. "How was your trip home?"

"Long and boring," Derek said. "But the summer was good—always is."

"Hey, how about we meet up on the Hill, and you can tell me all about it?"

"Ah, I'd love to, but I'm just unpacking. Anyway, after twelve hours in the car, I'm kind of beat."

"Tomorrow after school, then?"

"For sure. Back to St. Augustine, huh? I can't believe school's already starting. I just got home."

"Well, that's what happens when you stay on vacation till the last minute," Vijay pointed out. "Anyway, see you in class."

"*Seventh grade.* Unreal, huh?"

"I know. Crazy. Where did all those years go?"

"Really. Well, see you tomorrow." Derek hung up, and turned to find his mom standing there, her arms crossed and an amused look on her face.

"Seventh grade," she said. "You two are all grown up!"

Derek laughed, but in a way it was true. He did feel suddenly grown-up, or at least on the verge of it.

In other places kids went to different schools starting in sixth or seventh grade. He was still at St. Augustine, so going back shouldn't have felt much different.

And yet somehow it did. Derek actually felt more nervous than usual about the first day of school. The workload in seventh grade was rumored to be a lot harder. And it was definitely going to be weird going back to school and not seeing *Dave* there.

Dave Hennum was Derek's other best friend besides Vijay. But in June the Hennum family had moved all the way to Hong Kong. Dave's dad had been transferred there for work, and the family was going to live there for the next two years.

Derek wondered how Dave was getting along, with all his friends so far away, and him living in a strange new place, where people mostly spoke a different language. (Although, Dave had assured him that they spoke English, too.)

Derek hadn't gotten a letter from him for over a month. In that time, Derek had sent Dave three letters—not easy, considering he didn't much like letter writing to begin with.

During the summer he hadn't noticed Dave's absence much. Days at the lake in New Jersey with his dozens of cousins were full, noisy, and busy. He'd even gone into the city with his grandma a couple of times, to play ball with the city kids he'd met the summer before.

Overall he'd had his usual great time. He'd practically forgotten about Dave, except when Dave's letters had come—which hadn't happened since the end of July.

But now, back in Michigan and about to start school again, things already felt different. Not having Dave around, it felt like a big part of Derek's world was gone, and it made him sad in a way he'd never felt before.

Just then, though, Derek's dad came into the house, carrying a white plastic tub full of mail. "The postman was here and dropped this off," he said, setting it down on the floor. "I saw your name on one or two envelopes."

Derek sat down beside the tub and started rifling through the piles of envelopes, magazines, and catalogs—four days' worth, from the time when his parents had taken off in the car to pick up Derek and his little sister, Sharlee, and drive them home from New Jersey.

Soon Derek found the buried treasure he was looking for—two picture postcards from Dave, *and* a letter!

One postcard had a picture of a beautiful mountain, with skyscrapers crowding it from top to bottom. It was dated August 10—*four weeks ago*!

On the back of the card, Dave had written: "This is Victoria Peak, the most famous view in Hong Kong. We went up there on cable cars! It was cool, and a little scary. This place is amazing—very different from the States in a lot of ways, but the same in others."

That was it. There wasn't much room on the back of a postcard, after all.

The second card was dated August 15. It showed a beautiful golf course with a pagoda in front of it, and the same mountain, but in the distance this time. "This is the best golf course I've ever played," Dave had written on the back.

Golf was Dave's passion, in the same way that baseball was Derek's. That's why the two of them had always understood each other so well.

The rest of the postcard said: "My dad's company pays for his membership in the club, so I've already played there five times—in just three weeks! It's a hard course, but I love the challenge!"

Yup, thought Derek, smiling and shaking his head. *That's Dave, all right.*

But it was the *letter* that Derek wanted to see most. Pictures were one thing, but he wanted to know what it was really like for Dave, being in another country thousands of miles away from America.

Derek couldn't imagine himself in that kind of situation. He hadn't moved since he was four years old—and he had no intention of moving again anytime soon!

The letter was dated August 25. It read:

Dear Derek,

Well, I finally have time to sit down and write to you. You wouldn't believe how busy it's been! I have Cantonese language classes after school-yes, school! They start here at the beginning of August! Can you believe it?

School is harder here than at Saint Augustine, and the teachers are really strict too. My parents are always busy-my dad at work, my mom with starting up her own business-so they don't have much time to do stuff with me. And Chase isn't here, so I haven't had too much fun, other than golf.

Chase had been the Hennum family's driver and had often been in charge of watching Dave, since Mr. and Mrs. Hennum were out working most of the time. But he hadn't joined the family in Hong Kong.

Derek noticed that Dave still referred to Kalamazoo as "home." *Good.* That meant he still missed his old life, and his old *friends.* . . .

The best times I've had here are on Sundays, when my parents and I go touring around the city and the harbor. There are floating markets, where it's crowded with boats, all loaded with stuff for sale. We brought home all kinds of foods we'd never seen before, let alone eaten! Most of them taste good, but some are not so great to look at—I'll leave it at that.

Derek had to laugh. Dave's sense of humor had obviously survived the trip to China.

But the worst part is not being *there*, with you and Vijay and the rest of the kids, hanging out on Jeter's Hill and playing ball, hitting golf balls at my house. . . . You know, all that stuff. I get sad sometimes, but I'm sure once I make some friends here, it will get easier.

Well, I guess that's all for now. You'll be starting school soon, so at least I won't have to be jealous anymore, ha-ha.

Your friend,
Dave

Derek put the letter down on the table, next to the two postcards. He sat there thinking about what life was going to be like without Dave around. It made him feel at least a little better to know that Dave missed him too.

But not *that* much better. Not as good as if Dave were still in Michigan.

"It's the bottom of the ninth, two on, two out, with the Tigers trailing by a pair, 3–1. The first-place Red Sox have won five straight, and they're looking for more. . . . Carsten takes a fastball for ball one. . . ."

"He's gonna drive 'em in," Derek's dad said confidently, as Carsten let ball two go by. "You just watch, Derek."

Derek looked at his father sitting in his armchair, while Derek and Sharlee shared the couch, and Mom occupied the rocker in the corner. "How do you *know* that, Dad?"

"Don't believe me," Mr. Jeter said, a smile curling one corner of his mouth. "Just don't say I didn't warn you."

On the next pitch Carsten walloped a line drive into the right field corner. The runner on second scored, and the runner on first was rounding third. Derek and his dad were both yelling "Go! Go!" Sharlee got up and danced on the couch, until Mrs. Jeter told her to quit it.

"How did you know, Daddy?" Sharlee asked. "How did you—"

But Mr. Jeter wasn't listening. He wasn't smiling either. Kurt Carsten had pulled up lame before reaching second base. The throw came in to the second baseman, who tagged the limping Carsten out *before* the second runner crossed the plate.

Game over! Somehow the Tigers had snatched defeat from the jaws of victory!

"Well, that beats all," Mr. Jeter said disgustedly. "Why didn't he just stop at first if he was hurt?"

"Why would he do *that*, Dad?" Derek asked. "It was a double all the way."

"Because he's nursing a hamstring injury, that's why! You don't go full-out if you're protecting an injury. Not only did he cost us this game, but now he's going to miss a *bunch* of games—just watch—and for *what*?"

Derek was puzzled. He'd always played baseball full-out, running as hard and as fast as he could, diving for balls even if they were way out of reach. He couldn't conceive of a player holding back the way his father was suggesting!

They watched as Carsten limped off the field. "He already missed two weeks with it last month," said Mr. Jeter. "Now he's going to wind up missing half the stretch drive, and the team's going to have to catch Boston without him!" He shook his head. "He should have just sat on the bench and rested it every few games. But not Carsten. No, no—not him."

"He's their team leader, Dad! He's not going to sit down when the team needs him," Derek pointed out.

"And now the team's not going to have him for a longer period of time."

On the TV the on-field reporter caught up to Carsten just as he was about to hit the dugout. Mr. Jeter stood up.

"Where're you going, Dad?" Derek asked.

"I'm going to go grade some papers. This team drives me crazy."

"But, Dad—"

"Kurt," the reporter said, *"what happened out there?"*

Carsten shook his head sadly. *"I think I just pushed my body too hard."*

"Do you think the manager should have rested you longer?"

Carsten shrugged. *"I don't know,"* he said. *"We're in a pennant chase. I leaned on him to put me out there. So I guess that's on me."*

"You're the team leader," said the reporter. *"How are your teammates going to catch Boston now?"*

"I want to be out there every game, every inning," said Carsten. *"But we'll see what the doctors say. Even if I'm on the bench, I can still bring my energy to the dugout*

every day and cheer my guys on. If I can't set an exam-
ple with my game, I can still notice things, and pass them
along to my teammates—participate from the bench."

Mr. Jeter shook his head in dismay. Then he turned to Derek. "Did I ever tell you about when I hurt my knee in college?"

"Uh . . . a few times," Derek answered, looking from his mom to Sharlee. All of them had heard the story more than once and were trying not to laugh.

"Well, learn from other people's mistakes, Derek," said his dad, wagging his finger. "If you don't take care of your body, it won't take care of you."